I0769212

# DRY THE RAIN

### RICHARD LEISE

*For Adelle*

This is the definition of my life

— THE BETA BAND

I could tell you what He did in the beginning. After I finished drying the rain and the grass was still soaking wet, I could tell you how He would say, Come here, and how He would go and punish me. I could tell you all about the different ways He would hurt me, or the four or five ways He had of teaching me things, and you would be fascinated. Or maybe you would feel bad. Or you might even become horrified. Or you would find this to be just about the craziest thing you have ever heard and you would pick up your phone and talk with your friends about what had happened, you would text your texts and you would post your posts because *Dry The Rain* is based on real and actual events.

I mean, you would type, that could have been me. Or, your friends would say, it, by which they mean me, could have been one of my friends.

Can you imagine?

Isn't it the worst?

Or you might get bored. Who hasn't seen this story before? And you might change the channel. But no. You will keep watching because there is never anything on, at least not anything good, and besides, you would tell yourself, everybody else is watching. Something good might come from this.

But you, by which I mean the worst of you, woman or man, boy or girl, you would roll your eyes, you, just as a for instance, a certain sort of you would tell your girlfriend how the show was written to look a certain way, because what happened really did not happen, at least not in that way, the way they show it on *Dry The Rain*, because how could anyone know? Also, your boyfriend would say, these sorts of shows are made to make you feel sad and scared only to make you feel better by the time the show's over. That's why every movie has a happy ending, he would say. Even the new and the modern shows have at least for an ending something that leaves you feeling not bad. It is this agreement they make with you. The producers and the writers of these shows and these series. You watch and you feel terrible until you do not, and then you feel strong and then even stronger, like you have done something other than watch a TV show or movie.

The weak revenge. The strong forgive. The intelligent ignore.

That, your boyfriend does not say. Which is to say he is no Einstein.

It is, your boyfriend would say, by which he means watching *Dry The Rain*, kind of useful. At least in a way.

And remember, your boyfriend would say, the two of you just lying there in bed, all comfy in Nautica, don't forget that she, he would go on, by which he means me, don't forget that she was just this little kid when she was kidnapped, by which he means stolen. She's not exactly this reliable source of information. I mean, he would say, that's how you know it's not real. That *Dry The Rain* is not true. What kind of girl would want to remember anything like that? And think about it, he would say. What kind of girl would be able to remember anything like that? All they need, by which he means the producers and the writers, all they need to know is just a little bit to make it interesting. And not even that. They have writers who come up with different, better, ideas. They just need a little bit, by which he means from me, so they can say *Dry The Rain* is based on real and actual events. She, he says, talking about me, is just the basic idea.

I am clickbait.

I am the trailer.

And, he would go on, which is to say your boyfriend, this being the second time the two of you have seen this episode called *Fight or Flight*, because you are waiting for the next episode, and that will not be on TV until Sunday night, that being the best way for the producers to make money. But also, he would add, even if he does not say so exactly, by which I mean in so many words, you are watching *Dry The Rain* because *Dry The Rain* really is that good, supposedly. And not just the story, but the way everything is colored and arranged to keep you interested and fascinated. Every time you watch there is something new to discover. Or there is something you will find based on what you have read online. You have fun finding Easter eggs. A second sort of story.

And, he would go on, by which I mean your boyfriend, he would say that if you really pay attention, like if you really clue on in, by which he means to what is happening as opposed to what you think might be happening, it really wasn't as bad as they, by which he means the producers and the writers, are making it seem. Remember, he would say, you're watching TV. Remember, he would say, *Dry The Rain* is just a show. He would say that it's all produced. He would say that it's all written. By which he means scripted. He would end all this by saying that all sorts of stuff is made up. How, because you are watching TV, it just has to be.


One of you might ask your husband why it was that I did not just get up and escape when He was away at work, or wherever it was He went at night, or during the day. Because you have seen plenty of these stories before. There is always a way to escape. You have even seen shows like that terrible whatever Kimmy Whoever show and how what happened to me can actually be made funny if you forget the horrible parts involving tuning forks and teapots. Or, even better, the producers and the writers can find a way to make those parts funny as well. Watching me in His backyard drying the rain for what on at least one episode of *Dry The Rain* is supposed to be most of a day you would not wonder, If. You would say, after taking a sip from your latte, There was a way out. To that I would say just because he is not right or just because you are not right does not mean that either of you are exactly wrong. I mean, look at me. Here I am. But go ahead and try to kiss yourself in the mirror. Go for it. Aim for your cheek. Your forehead. You will find that all you can ever do is kiss yourself on the lips.

Forget drying the rain, I would tell you. I would say this because most of you have never had your leg in a bear trap. I would say this because most of you have never had your hands in a bucket of rats. And I would say this because none of you, I am sure, has ever had, when learning, or being taught one of His very particular lessons, to choose between a butter knife and a steak knife.

On the MovieTrap series *Dry The Rain* Imogen Appleton plays Mallory. This is the name the producers and the writers came up with for me because Mallory, when you look this up in the dictionary, means sadness, and my name, by which I mean my real name, well, you do not even have to look that one up to know what it means. This is because my real name just means a month. One of the ones with thirty-one days, that comes and goes every year and so means, if you stop to think about it, not very much.

If her name, by which I mean Imogen Appleton, sounds like something you have heard before, this is because Imogen Appleton is that one kid actor who I guess was in that really popular movie *Valdese* that came out last year in the actual movie theaters. Most people do not know that the movie, by which I mean *Valdese*, is based on this really cool book called *Being Dead*. A novel. This being one of the books that I read when I was in the hospital. After I killed Him.

.  .  .

There are four books about me. And by books I mean non-fiction. From what the producers and the writers put together to create the MovieTrap series, this one extremely famous author, the French one who wrote the book about sex tourism, and other books about Muslims, is writing *Dry The Rain* into a novel. Writing books based on TV shows and movies is one of the many things that surprises me.

But by now you know this. The stuff about Imogen Appleton, I mean. Everyone thinks it is crazy just how much I look like her. Or just how much Imogen looks like me, is better to say. For starters, we both have that crazy blond hair. But it is more than that. We really do look like sisters. Or maybe it is better to say, by which I mean it is more precise, maybe it is better to say that she is more like my mother. In terms of looking. By which I mean appearance. Mostly, at least if you were to ask me why, it's because of our eyes. They are really wide and super bright. And they seem just like stickers. Like as if our eyes were planted on top of our faces. As if it is like we are china dolls. And so this makes us have this weird dimension that seems to go well with our heads, or faces, I guess it is better to say, that everyone says have this perfect kind of symmetry. Of course she does not have to look like me to be Mallory, but because she does it is powerful even if only because she does not have to do as much acting-wise. She can even do a little bit less.

Because now I am free, and because of how I happened to make myself escape, which was super brutal and violent, I have all sorts of fans. There are tee shirts. And you can get me in a Halloween costume. The FBI tells my parents that there is nothing they can do about an unknown number of fans being like Him. As in people who are not only just psychos, because there are a countless number of those, but psychos who are in ways that nobody knows, by which I mean can anticipate, directly dangerous to me. They say someone planning to steal me would be this rare thing, but that I should always be ready and prepared. Just in case someone tries to do something crazy. Trust me, I am. I have on me, by which I mean at all times, mace. And I carry something else, too. So I do what I want to do. More than any of this, though, I am older. Someone like Him would have to kill me before they got close enough to touch me.

I get mail which we throw out, but of course people post stuff, which I consider mail, online. Which, even if you quickly delete, of course means you are deleting something you have seen. At least part of. Many of you say that if you were me you would not go online. Or that, if you did, you would figure out this way not to look at the stuff you did not want to see. Or that if I do, by which you mean if I do go online, I have only myself to blame. What can I say? What I can say is that not all of it is bad. Not all of it is awful, and some of what you write is beautiful. By which I mean pretty and nice. And for that I say thank you.

Many of you think that if you were me you would not own a computer. Or have a phone. That you would stay away from a lot of things. And there you are correct. At least kind of. I know exactly what to stay away from, and pretty much how to do so. And I know, for the most part, pretty much where to look for those things I like. That is the best I can do. Of course many of you feel otherwise, but that is just not true. This is because for us nowaday kids, or, to be more precise, what you might call young adults, by which I mean young women and men, going online is like going outside. You basically have to. Otherwise you would be a hermit. But a new kind. A new form of person created from a strange and maybe even more powerful fear and or possible dislike of other humans. This is because we are not so different. We are all just people, and we all have that in common. But anyways. Them, by which I mean the producers, those men and the at least two women going ahead and picking Imogen. That is just fine. That is totally fine and okay by me. If I was a producer and had been producing *Dry The Rain*, I bet I probably would have done the exact same thing.

Had I been born not so pretty or even just average looking that would have been one thing. One day and not particularly on accident I saw, by which I mean watched, part, which is to say most, of that one movie about that really famous female serial killer, and the idea that they take this one really beautiful woman actor and make her look not so pretty so that she looks more like the actual killer makes watching that movie stupid and impossible for me. And it has nothing to do with acting. And I do not care about some not so pretty woman not getting to act in the movie. Like if a movie is about a gay person I do not think you have to pick a gay person for the part, because that is like saying that every cat looks like the same cat and that there is something about acting that is not important or that is not worth valuing. I do not get it. That is what I do not get because with that one movie it becomes more about Look at what they did to the actor than about the killer. Or, more importantly, about looking at what the killer did to the people she killed. Not in terms of how she killed them, but just the fact that she did. Which is to say kill them at all. And how those people had families, just like I have a family. And how they know not what they do. To us. Which, specifically, for me, has to do especially with my Uncle Billy. How what He did to me made what used to be so easy for my Uncle Billy, by which I mean in terms of being around me, so hard. At least in the beginning. But I also and definitely mean to all. By which I mean even you, too.

Here is a point which is lost. The producers of *Dry The Rain* would not have made, were I not so pretty, a pretty actor look not so pretty. This is because creepy men and I suppose women watch movies and TV just to watch little kids in movies and on TV. A gross point of fact that is not lost on the producers. Mallory was going to be pretty to look at. Or maybe there would be no Mallory, by which I mean there would be no *Dry The Rain*, were I not so pretty. Perhaps my good looks gave the producers and the writers their idea. Anyways. There are plenty of not so pretty actors who would have been just fine, is what I mean. To act the part of the lady serial killer I was just talking, by which I mean writing, about. Or me, were I not so pretty.

But with *Dry The Rain* I definitely and totally agree that the actor should be pretty one way or the other, even if she did not look just like me, and that it might have been better had she not been Imogen Appelton but maybe someone even prettier, by which I mean lovelier, which is not an easy thing for me to describe the difference of or between. But I will try. Someone who is lovely is a person who shines. And if the person playing Mallory, which is to say me, was shining, this would have got at something that I have not told anybody and never will.

The producers got the basic part right though, and by this I mean having Mallory be pretty, because this is all that basically matters. This is because if I learned anything, if He taught me anything, by which I mean I learned it myself, like the way you learn when you read something, it is the true nature of beauty. Its power. And what I hear people call its allure. I can definitely say that I have found, and still do find, certain guys to be what I consider handsome. I am not sure I could put anyone on a scale from, like, one through ten. But like saying one thing is heavier than another, I can tell you that one guy looks nicer than another, and that some guys must weigh a ton.

Being beautiful for a movie star like Imogen Appleton makes her an object like a very old and rare painting that, by which I mean who, because she makes all sorts of money for other people, means that she also makes a lot of money for herself. And that for her, just like me, being so pretty means that people just want her. A lot of people. Or, if they cannot have her, they want to be around her. Or another person just like her.

You do not have to be movie star beautiful for that, though. And obviously there are way more beautiful people than there are movie stars. This is because there are not enough movies and there are not enough roles. And also, just to point out the obvious, this is because acting is not easy. It is hard. But there is more to it than that. Just like for me, how being very beautiful is what not only kept me alive and breathing, but also free from way too much of the really messed up torture stuff you do and especially do not see on the other TV shows, series, and movies, or especially hear about on podcasts, by which of course I mean any of them but the *Box of Rain* podcast especially, by which I mean in particular, which is only about Him and me. That podcast is different. This is because it does not really focus on what happened to the other girls He stole before me, who I'll talk about later. Which is of course very important. But not so much if you are only into *Dry The Rain*, or want to make money in your own way off of what happened to me. And because *Box of Rain* does not, I will. Talk about the other girls, this is to say. By which I mean in a manner of speaking.


When it came to catching and stealing little girls, He would have taken anything. This is because this is what He did. The way that little kids take care of Pokemon cards. Or old people go on and on about their colonoscopies. Which is to say religiously. And by that obviously I mean the ones He could catch. He would not just keep anyone, though. Of course the producers and the writers do not get into that at all, because there were only certain things they were interested in. And by interested in, I mean when writing things down while also of course taping, by which I mean transcribing, or, to be more precise, making copies of what I said. Which, given I never spoke, by which I mean what you would consider verbally, was, even I have to admit, necessary. Stuff for their version of me. By which I mean Mallory. Them knowing and then planning what you want to watch. What they know you want to see. The very and exact definition of deliberately.


I have not watched the whole entire series of *Dry The Rain*, but I have seen plenty and have read enough to know that when you watch *Dry The Rain* the show makes it seem like everyone He took was very pretty and quite beautiful. Or at least what you would consider nice looking and cute. Or at least not not so pretty. The producers' way of thinking, even though they did not say this, is, Who is going to want to watch, and for hours at a time, some not so pretty kid? Which also means, Who is going to feel bad for some not so pretty kid?

Or maybe, to be fair, they thought that you all will feel even far more worse for the pretty little things. That basically innocently or in some other way, they do not care so long as you are watching, they think you will want to spend more hours looking at pretty little things on TV, and that you will be more interested if He only looked for girls like me. By which I mean girls who look like me. Like if that was part of His hunting strategy. What you might call His M.O. Because people, even though this is totally not true, connect beauty and prettiness with wealth and money. Which means that all of the girls taken will be more interesting, that all of the girls will have, just like me, come from pretty interesting families. If not wildly interesting families. And that is just not how He was or how He worked. After all, you have seen the real shows. True, those True Crime shows may not be totally and exactly true, but the faces of the killers and the faces of the people they killed are. By which I mean you see exactly what everyone looked like, and you learn precisely where they came from. As in this is based on actual photographs and facts. And if you pay close attention to these shows you will see that they really only ever use one photo. By which I mean of the person who was killed. Or the person who went on to become a killer. Just one or maybe two. Which is weird. But which is not weird once you get to know producers. And how these shows work.

But all of that is obvious and not even interesting. And since learning about how the show is going, and what you all are seeing, I have been left wondering about a few things.

Like how they will show that a square will, in time, fit inside a circle. Or how will they show that eight-year-old girls, no matter what they look like, have two circles that some men find fascinating. Even though I try not to think too much about stuff like that, what can I say? Just like Him, sometimes your thoughts have you.

Maybe I will not have these thoughts once *Dry The Rain* goes away. By which I mean my thoughts will no longer have me. Or, to be more exact, I will have them. By which I mean I will have the thoughts that I want to have, and I will be in control. I will be free. Whatever that means.


When I first got home, which, by the way, was not as simple, by which I mean easy, as you no doubt think, I was not curious about anything. It was like being born without part of your brain, that part of your brain that makes you interested in things. I was and I still am afraid that in finding out something new I will lose something that was left, by which I mean something that remained a part of me from before He stole me, and because I do not know the word for this, I will say I was okay with what I had, which is to say the stuff that made me who I was, and there was nothing, other than my Uncle Billy, that I wanted so much that I was willing to trade. By which I mean give a part of myself away. However small it might seem. I will talk about my uncle later. Except for right now, which is to say this.

My parents and my doctor and the psychiatrists and the producers and the writers and many of you have it wrong. I am not hiding anything. There is not some big secret. I am just not that much to see. Uncle Billy knew this. Like me, he was happy to sit in silence. He, like me, because he spent time fighting what my parents called Overseas, lost part of his brain. Because of this, all those little things that do matter, by which I mean everything about me that people miss because they are too busy being sure they know who I am based on how they see, Uncle Billy did not miss. That is what made and makes him today so compatible with me. This, though, took time. By which I mean us seeing one another. What you would, and do call, reuniting. But believe me. Or not. As always, it is always up to you.

Sometimes when I was drying the rain bumblebees big as hummingbirds swooped and flit, they rose and they fell. They veered. They careened. I would stop and look at one and think, Smooth. Or I would stop and look at one and think, Angry. Then I would look and wait for a leaf to fall, and I would watch the leaf, knowing that what I was doing, by which I mean watching, I was doing differently. You have to be scratched many times before you learn to stop and watch to see how it is that your blood actually comes to the surface.

Uncle Billy knew this. By which I mean he had been scratched many times, too.

And not just that, but this. By which I mean this something about me that Uncle Billy just knew and would not forget or, as you might say, dismiss.

How to explain? I think what is important is not what I say, but how you listen. So here. It is not that I feel, but that I want to feel. It is just that just like a junkie I have developed tolerance. Of course I feel when I think, but, and this is not an easy thing to describe, I see my reason, by which I mean that I actually see what I am thinking, too. You can picture, if you want to, something like a yellow balloon. Only problem? You either cannot, or you refuse to. You only see the string. You ignore what is around me, and insist that my past is something I grab. That the past is what I hold on to. Like

Uncle Billy with his fish when he is fishing, I am happy letting what I think is too small go. I like watching my hand do nothing while feeling the string slide through my fingers and of course the balloon while, by which I mean as, it rises away and then floats. Higher and higher. How it gets smaller and smaller. Until there is nothing to see at all. But all you see is my hand. Holding on to that string.

Since everything, by which I mean since after I killed Him and moved back home, no one in my life has done anything wrong. It is just that in some ways some people will never be able to do things quite right. Like my mom. Standing next to my mom, with her happy smiles and slow bright and sparkling eyes, I feel safe. But I do feel. And in feeling, I go through, by which I mean experience, what psychiatrists call A proximity to being. And so while I really do not miss any one thing, I did miss not thinking about thinking. But getting bothered by that would be like getting mad at God. And then insisting that God doesn't exist. And so it is for this reason, by which I mean many others, that I particularly feel comfortable around my Uncle Billy.

For those of you interested in what is true, drying His grass was not the hard part. That was simple. Not possible to do, of course, but super easy. It is the ground, it is the Earth that creates so many problems. What happens is that when you step near the dried parts, by which I mean the areas I already dried with the towels, you push underwater water right back up to the surface. This basically makes it rain from the ground on up. Over and over. Again and again. Every time I took a step. Every time I sort of moved myself to stand still and settled my weight. Even if it was warm or hot out and the sun was helping, or better yet, even when it was warm or hot out and there was a breeze helping me, this did nothing about it raining from the ground on up. It did not take long to learn I had a problem, but it did take a long time to come up with a solution. I did not think I was exceptional. I did not think I was uncommon. But if I was anything I was aware of what I was and was not able to do. By which I mean I knew my limitations.

But I did. By which I mean come up with a system. A solution. And when I created this system, this way to dry the rain, I got great at drying the rain and I actually came to like it, at least of course speaking relatively. I am sure many of you are rolling your eyes. Some of you do not believe me, one, because you say you would never like, and by this I mean even relatively, anything He made you do. And then two, because this is nothing they show on the show, how can you know? All that I saw when I was at first curious and did watch the TV was me in this terrible way being satisfied. Which is different from being happy. Which of course I was, by which I mean satisfied, but that is only part of me, and it took a long time for that to become a part of me, and I certainly did not fall down to my knees and start crying, and my tears most definitely did not fall on the grass just as if my tears were raindrops that then needed drying. That me crying made drying the rain more difficult. That right there would be just one example of television being so stupid. So dumb.

And many of you of course would say there is no way you would ever get to like drying the rain. Or anything He made you do, so far as that goes. But for me it was just like anything that you have a hard time doing. Like maybe writing a long school paper for a teacher you don't like. Or for a teacher that you really do like, if you know what I mean. Or trying to learn German. Except for the once, I never tried to kill myself, and this is something they do show for real on

*Dry The Rain.* Or so I read. And the big reason for this, by which I mean me not repeatedly trying to kill myself, or even trying to kill myself more than once, is because I found things to like. Relatively.

The locks and the chains were my primary concern, and yes, I use concern like every other word, by which I mean on purpose, or what you would call intentionally, because after a while I just was not afraid. Well, I did worry that He was going to die, that He was going to die after He had locked me up some night, or for whatever one of His reasons might be, there, to this, by which I mean just when and for exactly how long He would lock me up, there being no reason and certainly nothing by way of rhyme, Him leaving me alone all locked up with no way to kill myself, and that I would just waste away into death and nothingness. all chained without rhyme or reason. If that did happen, I did not know what would happen. I just knew that it would not be good.

By now you of course know that He was even older than He is on *Dry The Rain.* His part being played by that one actor from that movie about monkeys, a famous actor who they also put on makeup or whatever to make him look fat and not so pretty. For some reason that is something I get because, one, he is a really good actor and famous and so more people will watch, and two, there is something different about beauty between men and women, boys and girls.

Anyways, He was older than even him, by which I mean the actor, and of course He smoked, and of course He got older every day, and He smoked more every day and every year He had me, and because smoking made Him sick and was making Him sicker, and because other than having me, smoking was the only thing that made Him feel better, He of course smoked more and more. Day after day. Year after year.

So yeah. That was what really bothered me. Dying without even having any sort of say. Chained to that wall with not even Him to help me. By which I mean to stay alive before He had a chance to kill me.

After I learned how to dry the rain, He needed to come up with a different reason, by which I mean reasons, to hit me. And no matter what you see on *Dry The Rain*, it really was not all that often that I would be what I consider beaten. This is because I was so pretty and He found so much of me pretty and He did not want to go messing up the way I looked and functioned, by which I mean how me and my body worked and looked, by which I mean biologically. Everything regarding beatings and even Him just hitting me at all after Episode Two, which has the stupid name *Fight or Flight*, is wrong.

At first, and for a while after He stole me, and the swelling went down and the bleeding mostly stopped, and most importantly I could and decided that I would and wanted to walk, and after He told me what to do about the rain after every time it rained, well, after He taught me a thing or two, I would take the towels and just, well, dry the rain. Many of you think that you would have had and come up with a better idea. Well then. Okay.

Anyways, it was not just the grass. The grass was just what you might consider ornamental. His backyard was small, not really any bigger than my mom and dad's wrap-around deck, but it was big to me. Huge, even. It would seem the same size to you, too, if you had to dry the rain. Plus, in case you have forgotten, I was just a little kid when He found me. Like I was in maybe the third or fourth grade. If even. This is easy to confuse because they only show me as older and getting older on *Dry The Rain,* because it does not matter how pretty you are. If you are too little to act you are too little to be taken seriously and no one wants to watch that. Well, not no one exactly. By which I mean you should know what I mean.


The area where He kept me was beneath His house. These eight really long and really fat steps cut out of rocks led to my room, by which I mean His cellar, and that was all made of stone, too. One other door opened. This was unlocked because through the other side, which was outside, that outside area was locked in by this really tall and really thick wooden fence. Things were this way because this let me get out to dry the rain even if He just unlocked the top door and called down and told me to go outside and dry the rain. Which of course was something that He did. And which of course was something I could do, because I was not chained up all of the time. I of course did not know this then, but the true clue telling me just how far away He, by which I mean we, were from other people and what you would call civilization, was this fence. It was not at all normal.


If you remember the trees behind the fence and how I described them, by which I mean how I will describe them, or how the producers and the writers show them, well go on right ahead and forget about them. By which I mean that if you can and are able to do so, think about different trees. If you can think about trees like they have out in California, those really, really huge trees with names that sound like Indians, by which I mean Sequoias, go on thinking about those.

The only way I can really use words to describe that fence now, because the fence really is pretty easy to draw, is to imagine in your mind a picture of one of those old forts the Pilgrims, when they landed here, by which I mean the United States of America, not necessarily but of course also Virginia, put up to protect themselves against the Indians. I know I should say Native Americans, but this is a point regarding words, or, to be more specific, language, I don't feel like getting into right now. Anyways. His fence was pretty much exactly like that. At least from what I can tell from the pictures in the schoolbooks they, by which I mean the government, or, to be more precise, the state, used to send in the mail to my parents, and from the computer lessons I was supposed to learn from online.

Basically though His fence was just like nothing I had ever seen. The back wall, which was the back of the fence and what I saw first when I stepped with my eyes all sore and squinty out from the cellar and into the sun to dry the rain, was forty cut down trees. One of each of their ends was buried in the earth like He planted them. You could see where their branches were sawed off, but you could also see where He rubbed them down so that they were as flat as pieces of paper.

Now before you go on talking about how you would have found a way through the fence, or a way to go over the fence, the really main thing to know is that these trees planted in the ground were squished very, very, close together. So close together was this wood that where they were rounded they were sort of pushed together to become flat as pieces of paper as well.

The other ends of the trees were sharp and pointy like the tips of super sharp pencils. Many of you think you would have been able to climb over them, that you would somehow climb a wooden wall five times taller than you are, a wall that is as flat as a piece of paper is thin, that you would have made a rope out of some material that was not even there, and that you would make like a cowboy a lasso and hoop one of the pencil points and climb your way right on up and over the top. Alright, then.

Why His fence was pointy is a mystery. This is because this was definitely unnecessary. These points, that is to say. Maybe He thought it was scary. Or maybe, like one of my first psychiatrists said, because she had nothing else to say because I was then, like now, not talking, maybe the way the fence looked made Him feel bigger, by which you might say superior, sort of like a king. I know what she meant.


I sure did not, and no other girl did either, carve anything into the fence, by which I mean marks for days or even just a picture. Or maybe something like your name. As if His back-yard was a cemetery and the trees were graves. You never knew what would make Him angry. And when you were outside if He was at home it did not matter if He was watching you or not, you were supposed to be drying the rain. But you could see where at least a few girls had tried to dig into the wood to make something to grab on to. Again, in case you forgot, He would be gone for who knows how long at work or shopping or wherever it was He went, and I guess they, by which I mean some of the other girls, thought they could work fast enough and dig deep enough to make enough marks to get them way up to the top. They, by which I mean the marks, were kind of like the opposite of those fake rocks you see screwed into those fake walls people use to practice rock climbing. And yeah, there were some rocks in His yard, and yeah these rocks were big enough to be tools, and no they were not big enough to be weapons to attack Him with but yeah, go on thinking and saying that you would have whatevered Him with a rock. Anyways, no girl ever got far. Because the marks they made were not deep. And they were not high.

That was the only thing I knew and that I can tell you for sure. That, and that He did not even try to fill them in. Seeing them pleased Him and made Him laugh and made Him smile and made Him feel good and maybe feel happy, even. No psychiatrist ever said that. I did.

The way His fence worked was something I never learned. This is something that they, by which I mean the producers and the writers, for sure would have wanted to have shown on *Dry The Rain* because it really was mysterious and the sort of thing you would not have seen or will ever see anywhere else in your lifetime. But they could not show you because I do not believe they had any clue. At all. Some things they, by which I mean the producers and the writers, just did not bother to think about. Yes, they had of course visited His house and looked it over from the top to the bottom many times. I know this because many of the times, by which I mean more than at least four, I was there, leading them around. Or should I say, to be more precise, I went wherever I was led.

· · ·

At first they brought with us what you would call, or at least I do, a sensitivity coordinator. This woman whose job it was to make sure none of the producers and the writers forgot I was what you would call traumatized and that I was this person, a girl, of course, who might, at any moment, faint, or possibly something even worse. But I will tell you, like I kept trying to tell them, I had only been in His house just that once. There was nothing for me to show. There was no way for me to tell. And His cellar. My Home. That, if you ask me, by which I mean of course they didn't, spoke for itself.

The woman, the sensitivity coordinator, this round, chubby little lady with super puffy and curly hair who, as a matter of fact, reminded me of a bird, by which I mean a pigeon, or maybe a robin, but a baby bird, by which I mean to say fledgling, well she was more nervous than I was. She was nice enough, I suppose. And I do not think you get that kind of job if you don't care about people like me, by which I mean generally. By which you would consider a matter of principle. So she did, by which I mean for real, and actually, she did, this woman, care about me, while the producers and the writers only cared about themselves, by which I mean they didn't want to get into trouble, by which I mean accused, of subjecting me to what you would call additional horrors.

People, I wanted to scream. Hello? I lived there. And this for even I don't know how long. I suppose you probably know. And I know some of my time might not match up, exactly, as I write these things, but this, by which I mean what I'm writing, isn't about that. By which I mean time. Getting everything just right so that what I say happened in your mind fits just so. Think of this, by which I mean what I'm writing, as the Bible. Think of this as The New Testament, to use the most precise and best what you would call diction. What I am writing is not some history book. Just like I'm no Jesus. This, by which I mean my story, is a sort of commercial. By which I mean advertisement. It's not like Matthew, Mark, Luke or John expected you to take them literally. And how they, too, were writing for particular audiences. Matthew, Jews. Mark, Romans. Luke, Gentiles. John, Christians. Besides, He was dead. So what was His cellar going to do? I know, I know. His cellar was going to trigger me. But while I am many things, I am not a gun.

When they finally got rid of her, by which I mean the sensitivity coordinator, who just made talking with the producers and the writers impossible because she would not stop interrupting everything, by which I literally mean everything, to make sure I was Fine or to ask if I was Okay, I would write them responses to their questions if I knew the answers and felt that it was an okay question or something worth answering. Sometimes, if I was irritated, I lied. I made other, crazier lies, when I knew they were getting irritated. Nothing too crazy to be unbelievable, I am not that creative, but some pretty good stuff. Me answering just enough to make sure they were happy was the important part. They never wanted to think I was not keeping up my end of the bargain.

Of course there were many things they did not discover because I only told them what they needed to know, and to make sure they were feeling I was keeping up my part of what I agreed to do, which to them meant talk. Show. And tell. Which obviously were details about my ordeal, by which I mean the way He did things. And how. And, especially, where. I told them what they wanted to hear. Or, at least, I told them what they thought they wanted to hear. Which you will just have to believe is way different from my ordeal. Or at least a different part of it. Which is what they always called it. It being what happened to me. My ordeal. Like just as a for instance. This is one very interesting thing. Past the pencil points of his wooden fence, by which I mean when, standing on my mattress in His cellar looking through my window, there, out in the distance, off to one side, which would be my left, was what you would call a coppice of something like birch, or maybe aspen. There were the tops of all these trees. Anyways, the area was regularly, by which I mean carefully, trimmed back to stumps. This, I know, was so that this continual supply of firewood could be brought into His house. I know, I know. How can a little girl, alone, in a cellar, standing on her mattress, have access to any of this exact information? At the time, of course, I only noticed there were less trees. That the copse, over time, wasn't as great as it used to be. When I went back, with the police, or with the producers and the writers, I saw so much more of what He was doing. By which I mean completely. And my thoughts were like puzzle pieces that, all of a sudden, just fit.

The trees surrounding this area grew to great heights. Its canopy made a shade of everything. Basically nothing or everything cast a shadow, which I thought was pretty interesting, and I could stand and stare at those trees and find so much to see. I learned where to find light, for one thing. Where it, by which I mean light, fell and fanned the ground. And when.

One day a deer walked across His backyard. The animal raised its head. The deer seemed to know where I was, by which I mean it looked at my window. I know, I know. The deer is on the ground. How is it that a deer, on the ground, becomes something that a little girl, in a cellar, standing on her mattress, comes to see? What I can say is this. He made a mistake? He had left His gate open for some known only to Him reason? Men like Him don't make many mistakes. Or not. Don't believe me. About the deer, I just can't explain. High in the sky, though, there was an airplane. There was no way to tell where it came from, or why. Just like that deer. I had nothing to do with any of this.

Anyways, there must have been a sound. The deer quickly looked. I knew that look. The deer lifted a foot so slowly. Slowly, or so I thought, I returned the look. I settled into my stance, by which I mean I was mindful not to move. Stance settled, I tried not to breathe. Slowly the deer lowered its head and sniffed the grass. And then it walked away.

The best way to build a myth is to tell the truth. This is what I do whenever I begin a story talking about my experiences from when He grabbed me through now, me sitting alone, staring out a different window, or, if you want me to be literally speaking, writing. This is because there is nothing more false than detailing a story about your own understanding of events as they happen to you, by which I mean of when to you they, by which I mean events, have happened. This is because at the beginning of any given thing, by which I mean event, memory, which may or may not try to correct itself, bends, it is pulled apart by what I consider and so have come to call worldly strings, and, once something stretches, it never assumes its original shape. This is why stories, good stories, are better told in the absence of truthful words. Exactness is something easily eroded, left, and I'm only using this word because I am remembering that deer, and its gray and black hoof, cleft.

.  .  .

I never again saw the deer, by which I mean any deer. I am not sure why this is so. Especially when you think about how much time I spent looking out that window. Out that window, right before the night, what I like to call the gloaming, I stood there, for hours and hours, staring. The trees without their leaves being blacker than the horizon and, thanks to perspective, its low, rolling hillside. Over the mountains and through the woods. How that provided the illusion of some life other than this, by which I meant that life I was living. I saw the trees like dead things rising from the earth with branches like claws reaching to claim nothing. Of course I couldn't see the branches. At least not really. That is not the point. Which is what I mean about telling the truth.

After I killed Him, I walked towards that deer. By which I mean where it had once stood. I made for those trees, by which I mean what was left of them. A route in the country I walked looking for something to access. There, between crumbling farms and rusty silos, old gas stations and home-made stands where, during the day, women and their children sold honey and jam, split-level houses and double wide trailers marked the roadway. There, atop gravel driveways, broken-looking SUVs and compressed pop-up campers, their tire cavities orange and rusty, their asking prices, scrawled black in permanent marker across rotten pieces of cardboard and stuck inside rain-stained front windows go on forever, unsold. And power lines, like cobwebs made by men, extended from telephone poles rising from either side of the highway to create a creepy, at least in my opinion, canopy.

I did not have the words for those thoughts, then.

Now, thoughts come to me more like words, and I have less of them.

Back then though, while walking, by which I mean barefoot limping, it was so quiet. Nothing, in this way totally different than before, seemed necessary. I passed giant billboards, their faces strips of peeling PVC, hanging from cracked open and damaged wood, the intestines of forgotten messages. In forgotten fields I passed broken barns, looking for everything like nothing. Stepping over a dead possum and how its end, the road, was just my beginning. This huge animal by my feet. This bloated corpse and how it was pushing against itself. Ants, thousands of ants crawled around a hole, or what you would call a cavity, and this cavity, or hole, was slowly made larger by such incessant purpose. Sunlight touched the points of so many jittering carapaces and made the insects something almost pretty. One bright mass.

And then just a bit of noise.

Birds calling from the tops of trees.

They were different sounds, these. Alarms. Birds warning one another that I was close, and getting closer. As if.

And so no, of course I did not bring anything up. Producers and maybe especially writers get really good at asking the exact wrong sorts of questions. There is no point in doing them any sorts of favors. But had they asked, by which I mean about the deer, and why, once I killed Him, I started walking in one direction instead of another, what I would have said was the truth.


Many of you think I wanted money. Many of you think that I wanted to talk about this and these other things. Many of you think that after I told them what He did in the beginning, that after I finished drying the rain and the grass was still soaking wet, you think I wanted to tell them all about the time I spent chained up, and about all the time He left me what you would call free, and all the things He did with a bar of soap. Or about the sink by my mattress. Many of you would say that I wanted all this attention. That I still want attention. You go online and post how for the rest of my life I will always be looking for ways to make your lives somehow about me. You will say that because I did not have any friends I had to do something to make myself happy, to make myself feel like I had friends. You will tell your friends how followers and friends are not the same thing. You would laugh. I mean, you would type, could you imagine being me?

Shudder, your friends would post.

And then they would add four of that one emoji with the blue head and the bright white eyes and the wide open mouth dark like a door, the shape of this face sort of like a light bulb and on either side of it those flipper hands.

Right? you would post back.

And you would add four of those skull and crossbones emojis. Whatever that is supposed to mean.

And I understand. For me, understanding that way of thinking really is easy. Because how can you know? By which I mean that you are wrong. It is my fault if I do not say anything. And I do not care what anyone thinks, me writing this is not to correct any of that, because this, me talking, by which I mean me writing, this is only because my mom and my dad have very sadly agreed that I should talk and say something, that it was the lesser of these evils I had to consider. And let me make this clear. Because even if it only matters to me, you still need to know. By which I mean read. My mom and my dad did not direct me to do anything. To them, I was not TV. They were way honest about having no idea about what they would do if they were me. So it kind of goes like this, more yes than less. By which I mean what they had to say.


One day they said they wanted to talk. My mom, who was very sad, said, and very matter of factly, with my dad just standing there next to her nodding, that this story, they never called it my ordeal, they told me, by which I mean very matter of factly, that this story, whatever it turned into being, was going to be made into a TV show series anyways, and that there was nothing we could do. And while they of course did not know yet about MovieTrap and the producers and the writers, they knew it would be something like this, or worse.

Forget the money, my mom said. She said, Put that to the side for a moment, because money makes everything confusing, and she said that I would never want for anything.

By which she meant I would always be taken care of. Which meant I would always have money. She never said this, but they had no accurate idea of how ruined I was, by which I mean generally. Everyone just assumed I was broken, and I knew they were prepared, by which I mean ready, to take care of me. Forever. But here is the thing.

I just was not that ruined.

I just was.

I was, of course, not normal. But again, I was not broken. By which I mean I didn't need to be put back together again. I was whole. I wasn't a bunch of parts that needed assembling. Like that possum. Like any variety of roadkill, a rotting carcass attracting pools of flies and large ravens brazen with bloodlust, a molten shape indecipherable until all but dissected, by which I mean studied, and even then a mystery often enough, only my entrails identifiable, lying there slumped and sloughing atop some road's shoulder. The girl He stole was not me. I had raised myself and He had not killed me and that was the thing. Of course I was different. But I didn't want to change. To become what? Who was to say. Certainly not me.

I had my parents. This is what mattered. And I had, when I needed him, which I knew could be whenever I wanted, my Uncle Billy. She, by which I mean my mom, said that what was important was control, and that if I wanted any control of what they, by which she meant the producers and the writers, said about what had happened to me, this was the only way. By which she meant me talking. Or, you could say, participating. And then because by now they were both talking to me in that funny sort of at the same time way they have, I knew they wanted me to talk.

And it is not just about talking, they said. If I did not talk I would have no way to protect myself not if, but when, they, the producers and the writers, made stuff up. Stuff that might not particularly bother me now, but might when I was older. By which I mean who knows when. Because age is just a number. Because, and this was about anyone, they said, no one knows how they are going to feel. Life is surprising like that. They looked at each other and smiled. There were tears in my mom's eyes. But she made it so that they did not fall.

They did not say so, but they, which is to say my mom and dad, thought I was too young to understand, so they kept on talking. Explaining things they did not have to explain. They said that if I spoke now and this was documented, I would have what they called recourse. Talking as if I did not understand what that word meant, which of course I did, my mom and my dad kept talking like I did not exactly get what they were saying and so they went on explaining. Of course I knew what they meant, but I do not want any of you confusing what I say or think with what other people, even if it is my mom or dad, have said or feel or think. I am my own person.

Then they looked at each other. Then they looked at me. And then my dad, as my mom looked at her hands, said that it was my choice, and they would understand either way, but when I was older I might care about the money and to not forget that now was not forever and that this, by which he meant that particular now we were then having, would soon be the past.

And then he said, Just like that time with Him is in the past.

And then he said, Even though He will be a part of you, forever.

And because they almost never mentioned Him, or that time when I was stolen from them, I knew that they thought this point was important. By which I mean as in very. My dad did not speak often. By which I mean now. As in this point in time since I have been home. Now, he is not being mean. He has just used too many words. When I was gone he used too many words trying to find me, and then, I know, the words he used to deal with understanding I was never coming home were just too many as well, and because he used so many words he is simply out of them. Which makes it difficult to not find, but to place yourself in a position to speak words. No. He is not one of those. He is not the sort of person like the doctors, the psychiatrists, the producers and maybe even especially the writers who speak words until they find what they want to say. Or an arrangement of words that, to them, is close enough. Unlike them, I understand and I love him. My dad. And so much of why I love him is because I understand.

·  ·  ·

Back then. In the beginning. By which I mean when I first was missing. They, by which I mean my parents, but my dad especially, told the police I was gone. The beginning was not long lasting. By which I mean they, my parents, were soon talking to detectives. No, my father insisted. I would never have run off. I was happy. The detectives believed him. They did not think my parents did anything. And this includes my dad and I know this because he had what many of you call a perfect alibi. He was at work. Surrounded by people he worked with. He, by which I mean my parents, were cooperative. They did not hire a lawyer. This, me going missing, was nothing like that. Of course as persons of interest they were at first considered, but they were never considered suspects. No one, not even any of You, has suggested this. Thanks.

Anyway, my dad went on. By which I mean now, after I had killed Him and was home and he had run out of words. He said how in talking about what happened I could in a way control what would soon be living a new past right now, by which he meant in this very present. He looked at my mom and said that because he thought I understood what they were saying, that it was worth bringing up that a lot of money, more money than I could right now possibly understand, might one day mean something.

I could always change my mind about the money, my mom had said. And fast. As if my dad, and so her, too, had made this big mistake. By which she meant I could just give the money away. Or just leave it in the bank. Which she explained was not exactly like not taking the money, but was close enough. They didn't use words like estate. They didn't say anything like trust. This was because they, when it came to the money, were unable to trust anything. Only, my dad said, that if I decided to say no, I could never say yes.

And my dad went on, he had said, While this is confus-ing, you can only change your mind about that, by which he meant the money, once you have it. By which he meant there would be no mind changing if I made up my mind not to take the money now. But it was not that confusing. I knew what he meant. I knew what my mom and dad were getting at. I knew that they thought the money was important. I also knew that they thought about the money differently. Or, to be more precise, that I didn't think about money. At all.

This isn't really worth writing about. But just so everyone knows. I know about what you call the inception. The begin-ning, by which I mean genesis, of *Dry The Rain*. And of course I know what I know from reading what I considered worth reading. And since I knew they, by which I mean my parents, loved me, that did, and does not, amount to much of anything. Despite the web sites. And especially because of the podcasts. I knew they thought a lot about me, and what was best for me, by which I mean not the worst, and that they were confused, and that they didn't exactly agree. About the money, I mean. But that is all that I knew. Because when-ever I heard them talking, and this about anything, I moved far enough away, or I went up to my room, so that I did not hear them talking. Trying not to argue. Trying to look at the same thing, similarly. But they both agreed, and totally, that, for one way or another, money was always important. And that money was only always unimportant if you did not have any.

Because they, by which I mean the producers and the writers, never really focused on His van except for that one time, they did not think to worry about how He parked. And because, remember, I was just one girl, and because I killed Him, they never got what you would call a confession. And because He never wrote anything down, by which I mean on paper or a computer, they only know of the girls whose body parts they found in and around His house. And even then they could really only know He was their killer because it made sense. There was nothing, by which I mean zero, proof. By which I mean evidence. They just had these really obvious clues. What you would call this incredible circumstantial evidence. As in, If He didn't leave those bodies there, then who did?

Not that I really cared, but they did have an inquiry, or something, regarding what He did to me. I think I understand why this matters, but I pretend I don't because this would lead to more questions. But regarding the other girls, He was not charged with any crimes. Yet. He is just considered this really big suspect. Which means that one day people might get justice, whatever something like giving out what is just, by which I mean what is right, and correct, to dead people and their living families, could possibly mean. But that is not my concern.

Anyways, His van must have been a clue. And a clue that He did use, and basically every day. But they, by which I mean the producers and the writers, pretty much ignored His van, because how would they know? They did ask me about it, and even though I kept a lot of secrets, I told them the truth about the van and that was this.

He left in His van basically every morning, He came back in His van basically every night, and He always wanted it dry after the rain. That, and of course some of the stuff about me and what He did to me when He first stole me. That was all. This is it. Relatively speaking.

. . .

Me not knowing anything, or at least me not knowing much about His van was because I do not remember much from that first morning other than after He grabbed and gagged me and then raped and then sodomized me and I did not faint but I was aware of so much of my body there was no one thing I could think of in any way at all and it was what I consider the most I had ever been. If you know what I mean. Not that I expect you to.

Not because He was nice, but because, like I said, He did not mean to ruin me and injure me, He was, in His way, gentle, and this, by which I mean using the word Gentle, is of course the one thing you talk about and use to prove that I am sick, by which you mean incredibly emotionally disturbed, or that I have some dumb syndrome, and of course you are exactly wrong because you are not thinking. He was being gentle. To Himself. This, like I have told you, is because of how good He thought I looked. Still. Because of the way He was leaning on me during these different points during when what was happening was happening, and because of how excited He was because I was new and looked so good, He was at one of those points where He could not control what He was thinking and so He also lost control of what He was doing and He really did hurt my throat and for a long time. Maybe forever. That it was not on purpose. This makes it worse.

Before Him, I never before thought about anything going inside me. That is the one thing that I guess I will never forget. And yes it hurt and very much so, but the fact that I could be ripped open and have things put into me was so scary it hurt me even more, and this in this totally different way that I do not have the words for. What if He filled me up with things that He did not take out. That was one thing that I remember thinking. This is one thing that you get to know because you are taking the time to read this. What if things started growing. That is another thought. And that is another thing you get to know. And therefore, just like Him, you are holding a part of me in your hands.

*Dry The Rain* does the exact opposite of this.

After He raped me, which took about as long as you would think, we were not in His van for very long. If you put a knife to my throat I would say I was always in Virginia, or maybe North Carolina, at the very furthest away. There is no way He drove us north to another state, I can say that for sure. Well, you know what I mean. But the rest is just a guess, there is no way for me to know. I never asked. And in all the time I was there I only left the once.


There was a way of opening the wood so He could drive in and park and keep His van hidden. But from where I was looking, which is to say from my side of the fence, there was nothing like a handle or a hinge or a track or a button, and so like I said it is still a mystery to me how He got that fence to open and to, of course, close.


Along with His van and the grass, there was His white plastic patio set and a shiny silver grill. Not that He ever used it, except for maybe a few times a year. Yes, I know. This, by which I mean the grill, could have been taken apart and its parts used as weapons. You would have used its parts as tools for your great escape. Well okay then. Sure.

· · ·

In the beginning, by which I mean after I started thinking about things like escaping, what I did at first before even thinking about drying the grass was start with the grill. Because its lid was sort of round the rain basically dried itself. This is because of gravity. And the wind and the sun when they were out and blowing they helped as well. I was too little to know why it was usually so windy and so warm. Now I know this is because I was so near the shore.

After the grill I moved on to the patio furniture. But this was just in the beginning. As I grew older or time passed or however you want to think of it, I thought to gently tip the furniture first, to push the chairs and the tables over onto their sides. And then I thought about lifting the grill. This let most of the water that was there in small individual puddles on the grill and the tables and the chairs fall off while I was drying other rain.

Behind the fence there were, like I said, huge pine and other trees. They grew way up high into the sky, those trees with their flowers big as human heads. By which I mean magnolias. Looking up I would have memories. And I do not mean sarcastically or anything. I am being honest and for real. I did not like memories. Like, at all. All they did was make me sad. And sadness, I learned, by which I mean felt, made me weak. So after a while I rarely looked up. I know many of you do not believe me. What else did I have, you think, except for my memories? Or, you tell your friends, what kind of person does not want to think about her family? It did not become for me, and this includes memories, about having things. This is one thing that many of you will never understand. And this is one thing, because of what *Dry The Rain* is, that you will never see. Besides, there was way much more for me to gain by studying the ground. There being no answers in the tops of trees.


Pinecones were all over His yard. I did not and still do not like the way they look or the way they smell. Even worse, they get white and sticky. I hate anything white and sticky. Still, I would pick them up and toss them over the fence. One less thing to dry. And besides, I had to dry the grass beneath them anyway.


A game I got to playing when I knew that He was not around was to throw the pinecones at the trees, the idea being to get them to land in the boughs and as high up as possible. Like I have told you, He was not home a lot and I now know that this was because He worked so much. Since killing Him and escaping and being reunited with my mom and dad I have been as far north as New York to visit the Hudson Highlands and there, tall as anything, are His same exact backyard trees. I have also been down to Georgia and Alabama, and I have seen the same exact trees. They follow me. Not like I have matured and am blooming, and not anything dramatic like I am falling apart, but more like I have a tear and am full of seeds which fall depending on how I am standing. By which I mean is how I now see things. By which I mean what He put in me does grow, in a manner of thinking. But, in that same manner of thinking, I am the sun. And so most of what He planted I can kill, and quite easily. I don't expect you to understand what I mean, but you can, by which I mean understand, if you really want to.

So now I know that His trees were not even really that tall. When I close my eyes and concentrate, I would say His particular trees go up about maybe forty or fifty feet into the air. Tall, sure. But nothing as tall like the great trees I have since seen. And one day plan to see.

His trees. How their branches spread in every direction and like they were broken off and stuck back on again they were bent and sort of twisted and misshapen. Like a bunch of crazy Q-tips. They were fun to consider. Which by fun, by which I mean all things being reconsidered, it was something to do. Like clouds, I saw in them, which is to say the branches coming off from the trees, different things. Things like turtles. Or Chinese dragons. It was that sort of thing.

The green of the pine needles was extreme. What this did was to make the wood, by which I mean the trunks and branches, look really brown, or even sort of gray, and from where I was standing the bark looked to me like scales, or maybe something like cracks in really dry ground, what I would now call fissures. The very green needles were not long and they came sort of bundled together as if they were wrapped. Those did not fall to the ground too much unless a really big and especially windy storm upset everything.

The pinecones when they were closed were skinny and curved kind of like those little bananas you see in some stores. And yes, just so you do not say I am ignoring this, they look like penises, or, as you would say, dicks. But what, I would ask you, does not look like a penis, or breasts, by which I mean tits, to so many of you? Anyways.

Like flowers in the sun over time they, by which I mean the pinecones, bloomed to become bigger and round like eggs. Like their trees, the opened-up pine cones had scales and every scale had a hard and exact sort of thorn as long and sharp as a cat's claw. I considered it cheating to pick off the thorns before throwing them as high up as possible into the boughs of the trees, so my hands got pretty tough over time. Even now you see on my hands a lot of little white scars, and people have the completely wrong idea about them. This is something I keep to myself, because most of the time I have learned it is just easier to let people think what they want to believe.

One good thing about the thorns was that you could let one get stuck into your pointer finger just this little bit and at the end of your throwing it, by which I mean the pinecone, use your finger to sort of push free the cone and it would spiral like a football thrown by some NFL quarterback, and while I am sure many of you do not believe me you are right in that this did not help with aiming. But it really did help with me throwing them further, which is to say higher. The trick, and this is too hard to explain, but the trick was to get the pine cones so that they both sort of spiraled and tumbled end over end. The tumbling is what really helped with how I would aim and, more importantly, in how I would get the pine cones to actually land. To get the pine cones back up in their trees.


You probably think this game is made up. You, you say, just wrote about how I don't like looking up. That I'm contradicting myself. But you say a lot of things. But what I will say is that the last time I played the game and when I considered it over and I told myself that I won, I threw ten pinecones way high up and into the air and into the boughs of His trees and not one fell to the ground. And more than any of this, they all landed right where I wanted them. Well of course in that manner of speaking. As in more yes than less. As if I climbed up those trees and placed those pine cones exactly so.

I hear your sighs.

I see the bright whites of your rolled up eyes.

But what I do not hear is you asking yourself Why? Why would I care to make this up? Why, about pine cones, would I lie? If you were smart, you would say that I thought about and made all of this stuff up instead of having or thinking about my memories. While this is not true, you, if you were smart, would post this, or something like that, online. But you do not post this online. And this is not something you say. If you were smart, I would just say, As if there was a point to that. Like, what did I have to gain? And if you are smart you should be asking yourself why I considered the game over and why I told myself I won. You should post, Who was I playing against? For which the answer to that question is that because like any game it does not become a game until there is a way to win and a way for it to end, and I wanted to play a game because looking for a hobby was not exactly an option and Hey, is not solitaire a game too.

That is okay, though. The producers and the writers did not care either. About my game, I mean. For whatever reason, this means much more to me. And concerning me, and reason, they are not all that interested. By which I mean they have their reasons. Conversations which, while about me, have nothing to do with me. Sure, my game is part of the show. Only instead of simply showing what actually happened, they decided to show me cutting myself, which, if you ask me, is just a plot hole because why would a little girl like me do something like that when there was a guy like Him just waiting to freak out if He saw on my body some sort of injury other than anything He created? A Him who freaked out if He saw on me and my body an injury that even

He created? Or why would Mallory, by which I mean me, have done something like cutting? Cutting is what my psychiatrists call one of those innate ideas, something that a little girl like me would suddenly just do. A coping mechanism. Pain. To deal with pain. Sure, that makes sense now. But what do I know? Maybe as much as any other human being. Which by this I am talking about knowing things innately, I mean. Anyways. The producers and the writers no doubt saw the scars on my hands and one of the writers dreamed up cutting.

And it is not just the producers. And it is not just the writers. No one listens to what I have to say. But the joke is on them. And while of course I mean that sarcastically, they actually are laughing. By which I mean, to use another cliché, all the way to the bank. My game is not only this social media challenge that went, and still is viral, PainCone, an app which I have not downloaded but kind of want to, is the world's most popular free-to-play game. Like I said or will soon write, my mom has a great agent. So we are, to coin just one more phrase, rolling in it.


What I will say about it becoming easier, though, which to be clear, is me talking about throwing the pinecones way up high into the boughs of trees, is that aside from the obvious fact that I often practiced, this, my game, me throwing the pinecones for real, or when I was practicing before getting started, was always after the rain.

You are no doubt saying that Of course. What is she talking about? That is as obvious it gets. You are no doubt texting that of course me being outside was because I was out there to dry the rain which, of course, meant it just rained. To which I would say two things. One. It just stopped raining. And next, well here is the thing you do not know and probably cannot possibly understand. I only dried the rain when outside it was beautiful again, when there was literally no chance of rain and the sun was high and the sky was blue. As if in one of His weird ways He did not want me to get in any other way wet. Other than the two very particular ways He went about getting me how He wanted me. By which I mean wet. By which of course I mean gross. Totally.

Or maybe it had a different sort of meaning. Him letting me outside only when it was completely and totally beautiful. You and me do have this in common, I can say that much. We will believe what we want to believe.

He never came to care about me. This just is not true. I have read some of you talking about and guessing and posting ideas like His wife or His family left Him or were killed in some horrible car-crash fire and I came to represent that, by which you mean His wife or His lost family or His daughter or some weird combination of both, and so in a way, you say, or you post, He is, while sick, sort of tragic. Like Frankenstein. By which many of you mean someone else.

But no. For real. None of His behavior or the way He acted, other than maybe getting older, or unhealthier, had anything to do with me surviving and my killing Him or had anything in any way at all with How he thought about me and How he treated me. Which was to say pretty much always the same, other than, as I have already said, He started beating on me less and less, by which I mean instead of more and more.

So no.

Think what you want, but He felt nothing for me. If He was some kid and I was a cat He would have put me in a pillowcase and set me on fire and thrown me into a creek. Or if He was this teen and I was a fly he would have ripped off my wings. He would have looked down on me and said, Try and fly now, fly.

And no. There is nothing symbolic in that. In any way. By which I mean at all.

So no. Not in that normal human being way did He ever come to care about me. So it was as it would forever be, which by that I mean it was impossible for Him to be kind. It was not possible for Him to be a human being. By which I mean a you. Or a me.

The only thing He was capable of being was more in control. Or less out of control. Depending on how you want to look at it. So all that I can say about me being let outside when the weather was wonderful, the sun warm on my skin, the smell of a world other than cellar and cement and just as bright as any perfume, is that it was just one of those things.

Imagine His backyard was a window. When He let me outside it was as if my eyes looked through this crystal clear glass to see in front of me what I some days thought of as a painting and, on other days, a photograph. Of course there were trees, but I could dream of a world without trees, without a fence and without anything. Do not ask me why but sometimes, when my mind was working a certain way, this, what I now call my wasteland, would start to bloom, by which I mean whatever it was I imagined began blossoming. Whenever this happened, or whenever I let this happen, from the ground a rainbow of color rose and there before me was a desert. This was when the world was more like a memory. This was when the world became something like, to be more precise, which is something I can be, when I care to take the time to be so, by which I mean I have all sorts of words and know just how to use them, by which I mean not just exactly but savagely, which is something you will get to see if you keep reading, a painting. A painting whose colors were my dreams. My desert was dry but was very much alive with a wide array of succulents and cacti, of wildflowers and those great very sharp and green grasses like you find at the beach and all of it glossy like a magazine, the yellow flowers atop the Barrel Cactus, the bluish-greens of the Juniper's seedlings, the fat, blobby reds of the Desert Christmas Cactus, the gray smear of the rising Century Plant's basal rosette and when I looked I saw how all of it amazed, just as if the sun was a crayon making everything a bit more yellow. Then, at least some of the times, the sun came even closer and melted every yellow petal and ruined every blueberry and fried the red flowers and made something like leather, or a kind of jerky, of those evergreens.

Sometimes there were trees, though. And when there were trees the trees would make outside the window this foreground where otherwise there was nothing, where otherwise there was just all of this unnamed distance, what I considered the skin, or the flesh of the surrounding desert, and this all bumpy with wind-blown dunes, dunes which rose and fell like the far out low-lying hillsides, and these hillsides the color of wet paper, the desert also this strange sort of shadowy darkness and sort of moving like those waves you, on really hot days will, if you squint your eyes and tilt your head just right, see smoking on up from the street.


I was never outside at night. Or, if I was, I was not out for long. The reason for this, like so much, I do not know why. There is no way to even really guess. But there was this one time. Later, much later than ever before, by which I mean after the sun had sunk below the hillside, color, by which I mean this bright turquoise blue, made of the horizon one bright line. Where other than grass and pine cones there was not anything, just nothingness. Where all there was was just that wall of wood and beyond that through the trees there was this line of color that split the world in half. It did not have a name and it should not have a name. Out there in what is the direction opposite the ocean, where come fall the leaves of the trees, like skin on all of these fingers of fire, and how the hills turned gold like windy dunes, the rise and then this fall of the not tall hillsides and these hillsides dark and filled with shadows and the ground was like these ribs from which they rose and what I want to know is did I think that way, by which I mean about me imagining the desert, because of what I saw every day, or did what I see somehow make it possible for me to dream? Anyways.

At the end of long days the hills were dark like paper dipped and pulled from water and they were wavy and there was a break, that part between the tops of the hills and the bottom of the sky like breakers at the beach and all of this was pretty but this beauty was of this really quiet and silent kind. The beauty was able, as if it were a TV, to bring to my mind something unreal but that was, for me, pretty and interesting and something that I really liked watching. Like how it was and of course must be for people in museums standing and staring at famous paintings. Some painting like the one of that park with tiny people in top hats and big dresses and umbrellas pointing and walking with their arms and legs all weird and straight and looking like little Monopoly men and set to hang in a golden sparkling frame.

That one night, though. The air was thick, by which I mean it was like this solid thing. I reached out before me and grabbed fistfuls of air. Everything smelled like salt. At first I felt, by which I mean I could just tell that the sun was setting. Of course I regularly saw this through my cellar window, but having this happen while I was outside was what you might consider a vacation. Soon, those distant hillsides would be erased and there would be no trees. Just shapes. Just these black waves like a black sea against a not as black sky just miles and miles away. Way at the top of one of these hills were four of what I called, by which I mean considered, light towers. I was told these are called broadcast masts. They reminded me, even though I tried to push away this thought, of these bright red nutcrackers my mom put out at Christmas.

There were four lights glowing on each tower. The lights sort of pulsed, or what I called throbbed, like how a wound, by which I should say injury, like if you are hit in the head or the vagina, sort of moves in and out, or up and down, with the way you breathe, or how your blood pulses through your body. There was one light at the top of each tower. One below that. One below that. And there was one more light below that. This was the bottom light, but of course it was high off the ground. The light towers, just like the nutcrackers, fell in terms of how tall they were. And the red lights throbbed slowly. The red lights blinked on and then almost, but not quite, off, interrupting the darkness. In a way they were like stars. Blinking on and then off. Blinking on and then off. I know they never stopped. By which I mean I know some man in some room did not flip a switch to turn them off. I know their light was only erased, for the day, by the risen and glowing sun.


The problem with English, and many of you are just going to have to take my word on this, by which I mean if you keep on reading you will learn how I know a little about a lot and a lot about a little, is that our words mean next to nothing. Like love. I love birds. I love my mom and I love my dad. But differently. Only we, by which I mean you and I who go around speaking English, only have the one word, by which I mean love, which, when it comes to birds and my mom and dad, or birds and my mom, or birds and my dad, or my mom and my dad, when I say, by which I mean write, love, I mean something different every time. Love is a concept. Love is an idea. Can you believe in Love? Perhaps. Maybe. We people certainly believe in much stranger things, like, just as a for instance, maps. But the concept, by which I mean the idea of Love, is what you would call ambiguous. The idea of being in love? This, if you take the time to look it up, comes around, by which I mean is first documented and written about, in the fifteenth century. That, to me, is crazy. Although, if I'm being honest, and I am nothing but, I suppose I don't know when I thought the words first came about. By which I mean I never before took time to give it, by which I mean the idea, any thought. Definitely by the time of the ancient Greeks, you'd think. But what do I know? Anyway. The idea of a love letter comes from the thirteenth century. The notion of human beings falling in love first appears in the fourteenth century. The phrase no love lost appears in the seventeenth century and was used to talk about two people deeply in love, as well as two people who had no love for the other at all. Love, if you're playing tennis, means nothing. So I mean, yeah. Really.


What am I going on about, you wonder. Well, that would be this. I, as many of you know, and think to be just this most outrageous thing, am religious. He, by which I mean Him, had a body. He had no soul. If He was anything, He was the sum of a series of fairly simple equations inscribed on His brain matter, if you can even call it that, at birth. Written by God, crazy as that seems. This strange geometry accounted for His being. Don't picture His brain as some pink, cartoonish emoji, but a grid. Black and white. Like the lie detectors' annotated transcript. Like what you see on screen when monitoring an active EKG. Like those waves when, following an earthquake, you read the Richter.

His birth had been the earthquake.

His childhood, the heart attack.

The present, a lie.

A strange orogeny, to use what you consider a fancy but what I know is the perfect word, was His brain, which informed a series of crests, or a minor, like what I saw when looking out my window, mountain chain. He practiced certain principles, by which I mean these were not peaks of thought, but, to use this metaphor, these minor mountains of being, imperceptibly shifting atop some invisible plane, in all of His affairs. By which I mean when it came to everything He did.

A writer I love said that the moral sense in mortals is the duty we have to pay on our moral sense of beauty. Apply what that means to Him. For Him the world just was not pretty. Like the wind, I could not tell you where a man like Him comes from, rises, or why. Not that it matters. It wasn't easy, but I made it easy. Thanks to God. Thanks to Mary. We flattened Him. We reduced Him to a very simple range.


Of language, though. Given that, while don't get me wrong, I am not saying I am some mystic, but because of what happened, which if you somehow don't know about you are soon going to learn, by which I mean read. But there's no way any of you don't know that I love reading. What, though, you want to know. Oh, this isn't easy to say. A lot about a little. And a little about a lot. I was drawn to Mechthild of Magdeburg and Marguerite Porete, whom you have never heard of, and I say their names only because this means, by which I mean quite naturally, I have come to read a great deal about Meister Eckhart and, by which you would call extension, the word Ground. For us, by which I mean ground, this was translated from a German word. It does not matter which. But, and this is what I, by which I mean you, too, should internalize, by which I mean come to understand, is how that word, ground, in German, has four different meanings. And how Eckhart uses all of them. By which I mean meanings, to get his point across concerning how God entered his life, he uses ground differently, in these four unique ways. Now from here I could go off on a tangent. But don't worry, because I won't.

But back to that night. Or the few nights like it. What was particularly weird was that there were no bugs, at least not really. There was just this chirring from whatever insects were way up high in those far away magnolias, those trees with those flowers big as babies' heads. There were bats and they fell and tumbled from the sky as if their flying was this great big accident. A cloud passed in front of the moon and my eyes adjusted to the darkness and the stillness and the silence, by which I mean the nightsounds, and how they, the sounds being made at night, made everything quieter than it was. Everything seemed to be its opposite, and far away there was lightning in the clouds, that sort of lightning that lives in clouds, and while there was nothing from them, by which I mean the bolts of lighting were silent, my mind invented their sounds. The blats. The booms.

. . .

When I invented the pinecone game, my hair was still short. Like that sort of bob you recognize from the pictures of me that make up some of the introduction of every *Dry The Rain* episode. Those pictures and that music, that one song from the one really famous singer with the *Folksongz* album. My family, by which I mean my mom and my dad, might have agreed to many things, and for all sorts of different reasons, but one thing my mom and my dad would never have done is give anyone any pictures of me from before I was stolen. And by that I mean not one. And this reason being as much for them, even though of course they were and always are thinking of me.

When you are watching the introduction. When you see how those lotto scratch off tickets are sort of scratched by that sort of invisible hand holding that gold coin to reveal different pictures of me? You are supposed to be thinking as if life were some sort of lottery and I am just one cherry. So sorry. Unlucky. Those pictures of me that someone somewhere somehow got a hold of and sold. That is the real me. Those are the only bits of me left that you can look at and see me as being not what you consider ruined. It really is true. And that man in the one picture with me, the one with the huge beard and the even greater smile? That, no matter how much you think we look alike, is not my father. That is my Uncle Billy. Which, again, only you get to know because you took the time to read this.

Now forget Imogen Appelton. Now forget me. I look like a different human being completely. You might not think so, but it is way creepy. Not that I mind at all. It would be impossible for me to understand how I would feel differently.

So why bother feeling. Many of you of course do not believe me, but it is impossible for me to mind anything. Even some of you. Maybe even perhaps especially you. What you think or are thinking. What you have said or are saying. I do not remember anything from before Him. Well, you know what I mean. There is this one thing. Or two. This is that one thing.

What I am writing here is important. You will eventually see. Do not get bored. Do not skip pages to read more, by which I mean faster, just to get to read different things about what He did to me. That will make you a You. By which I mean one of all the people I just do not get or am against. But to make this a bit more like those shows. Those terrible True Crime shows that use people's pain like commercials. By which I mean not to advertise, but to get at some part of you you fail to realize exists. And that wants things you do not even know you resist. You will soon read about the first time my mom hit me. And while yes, I admit, it's not as crazy as something about Him, it sure is something.


I did not know this then, but, like so much, I know this now. After me, by which I mean not long after I was born, my mother miscarried. This led to a hysterectomy. I did not know this then, but, like so much, I know this now. After me, by which I mean not long after I was born, my mother miscarried. This led to a hysterectomy. She was not happy, but she was lucky in that her hormones did not make her depressed. My mom was sad, but the chemicals in her body didn't drive her crazy. Still. There are things that happen to our bodies as little girls and even ladies that make it impossible for us to get up and move around for a while, especially when they involve those certain areas and special parts of our bodies connected in ways we find confusing until it is time to understand. And even then. So much remains a mystery. That is what happened to my mom. There are things that happen to our bodies as little girls and even ladies that make it impossible for us to get up and move around for a while, especially when they involve those certain areas and special parts of our bodies connected in ways we find confusing until it is time to understand. And even then. So much remains a mystery. That is what happened to my mom.

I did not understand it back then. I just wanted her back the way she was when she was home from work, which was exciting and fun and full of things to do and my days were made from the different parts of the magical and mysterious activities she spent time conjuring. It is hard to think back that far, but I do remember that I kept asking her to get up and I kept asking her why she would not get up. I remember her looking at me and smiling. I remember thinking she was tired, but I could never remember her being tired before. As in ever. I do not remember what she said. All that I do remember is that one day she did get up and all was like before. It is because she got up so suddenly that I so clearly remember that one day.

Like one of those dog toys, like two tennis balls at the end of a thick, fat rope. That is how we moved through the shopping center, or wherever we went, really. Me one ball and my mom another and how we were never further apart than that one distance, which was the length of the rope. Let me tell you what you are thinking. Let me write what you are saying and posting. If that was true, you are thinking. If that was true, you are posting. How, then, did I ever get kidnapped and stolen?

Well, I am sorry. But that is just one dumb question.

When I was little it was obvious I was pretty and was going to grow up to be a beautiful woman and maybe even glamorous. My mom was an anchor person on TV and everyone said I got all of her genes and if I needed any extra I could pull the best of the rest from my dad. He was just what most people consider handsome. There are, of course, those *Dry The Rain* pictures, but we of course have other pictures from times before that. Pictures that people did not steal and sell. Like when we were getting ready for one of the holidays. There are lots of those. Or from one of the many times when we were at the shore.

To look at those pictures is to see the huge and bright sun acting like a spotlight to make my hair basically burst and explode with color, my hair a corkscrewed flop that shot way past my shoulders and how it seemed dipped in sparkles and so it glittered all that much brighter with blond. Sort of like sand. That white kind of sand by that crazy blue water that makes the sand look even whiter. I had then, like I do now, legs that were really long and what you would consider lean. In these pictures, because of my genes and how much I played and because I got healthy food and so much summer sun they browned down to what you would consider cream and freckled ankles, my toenails always painted this version of pink that was shiny and brighter than bubblegum.

Doctors corrected my clubfoot during infancy, and unless you were looking to find something the matter you would never have noticed what people called a deformity. Because they do not ever bring up my before Him childhood on *Dry The Rain*, and because you are supposed to believe that Imogen Appleton is me, this part of my being alive means nothing, and makes how it was I was able to escape from the chains all the more confusing.

Or, as some of you would say, not true.

Or unbelievable.

And so I cannot believe the producers and the writers left that part out. Me having a clubfoot, I mean. Well, that is wrong. I can. This is because they, by which I mean the producers and the writers, were not interested in things like honesty. By which I mean accuracy. They, unlike people who have what you would call integrity, did not put *Dry The Rain* together from the idea that the truth of a thing is in the feeling you got from watching. And they did not have the idea that the truth of a thing is in the thinking about the thing. This is not that easy to explain. If there are ends, their means were simply to create whatever exists between feeling and thinking. And this was in no way necessarily that line from your head to your heart.

The producers and the writers left that part out of me, by which I mean Mallory, because what it does is it makes you not even bother to consider, by which I mean notice, the other part of my escape, by which I mean the religious stuff, because that, by which I mean the religious stuff, was written about and discussed so widely by people who hate *Dry The Rain* not because of the show, but because of the people who watch it. By which I mean people who are not religious. And so it really is possible that the producers and the writers think doing so, by which I mean leaving that part of me out of Mallory, that this will get you watching the episode, or that part of *Dry The Rain* again and again and again and again, because they cannot leave it out, that would be too obvious, but they can make it, by which I mean the other part, which I will explain later, seem stupid. And so you watch that part of *Dry The Rain* again and again and again and again because of how it is presented, which is something they, by which I mean the producers and the writers, never want to stop happening. So yeah. That is it. That has to be the reason why. But if I never cared what you think before, I especially care even less when it comes to Mary. I told them what I saw and how she helped me. This is true and regarding Mary I could not have been more clear. Because if I owe anyone anything it is Mary. And it does not matter what you, or anyone, has to say.

So like I was saying, going back to this one day that my mom finally got up. We were shopping. My mom did not care about anything other than my health and she was convinced, I do remember this, that as I grew up and got older my foot was going to hurt my back. Her point was that how I moved around as a kid was going to mess me up later in life, if I was not careful. So while she was of course worried about normal parent things, like me getting taken and stolen, she was just as worried about unique, by which I mean individual, parent things, that had only to do with me, me being totally and completely individual when it came to her being a parent.

Regarding worries that are normal, for instance, my school would give us Stranger Danger talks. They taught us that you could pick up any cell phone, even if it was dead, or broken, by which I mean it didn't have power, and you could still press Nine and then One and then One and the phone would ring and you could talk to someone. She, which is to say my mom, like any normal human being, did not dwell on those things. She figured that stuff was, more yes than less, covered. Of course it came up, but, instead, unlike a normal human being, at least the way I was seeing things, she spent all this time worrying about my foot, or what I considered my body.

If you don't start walking right, now, my Mom said, her face all squished and serious. If you don't concentrate every day you'll end up walking wrong, forever.

We were by the food court because of my dad. I remember we were there to get something for my dad's birthday, just to make this story, now, exactly as it was happening, then. My mom, because she was still not back at work and there was extra time all over her hands, was planning a party. My dad did not and still does not like attention, which is another reason why I remember this. As in what we were doing and why. As usual, I did not get the big deal. This I remember because my mom was always making a big deal about my foot. Just because I was stolen and all sorts of awful stuff happened to me there is no point in saying things differently about my life before there was a Him. A He. My mom could be so annoying. What was I supposed to do, I always thought. Think really hard and force my foot to grow? Concentrate so much that my left leg, my left calf, would fatten up, by which I mean become more muscular, and come to look the same as my right leg, my right calf, which everyone, including my mom, looked at as normal? Assuming anyone other than my mom was looking. Which I can tell you for a fact they were not. Not even Him, if that tells you anything. And it definitely should.

I did not think of it like this until I was gone and stolen, but my left foot was and of course still is much smaller than the other. To be exact, it is about two thirds the size of the other. Well, probably closer to seven eighths, but you get the idea. More importantly, my leg, which is to say my calf, was skinnier, also. I was not a starfish. My foot was not going to grow, by which I mean regenerate. However I walked, I planned on walking that way forever. And the reason for this was because this way of thinking of walking without thinking just worked well for me, or what I would now consider in my favor. Like I said, I walked about totally unnoticed. Most of this was thanks to my mom, of course. When we went shopping for sneakers my mom bought two pairs in two different sizes. So my shoes always fit. No one cared. There was nothing at all to see. Only my mom complained. When we spoke about my foot it was only for her to argue, and she always started it, and I was not a baby, and I really did know what I was doing. So I was lost in my thoughts that day we were shopping, by which I mean the day she finally got back up and started doing things. And then, before I knew it, I was lost, lost.


I do remember this. Strangers brushed past. Close by, on top of a brand-new car, which is always weird to see parked inside a building, instead of out, one of those boats designed to look like a kazoo, which of course I now know is a kayak, the silver specks in its green paint glittering. Off to one side a glass storefront. Behind the glass and standing on white boxes and white cylinders white like the color of milk were milk white mannequins staged in blue shorts and bright shirts, their heads and arms and legs cut off at weird angles.

I saw everything way more clearly because I could not see my mom, by which I mean all of a sudden, like a slap in the face, or being kicked in the stomach, and everything became much more intense and I thought about just one thing, which was that I was lost. When this happened, my mind shut down. Everything was erased. It was like staring at a light that someone suddenly turned off and I saw both light and dark and I felt a little bit dizzy. I knew there was nothing wrong with me and that I was just nervous and that I must stop thinking about being afraid, that otherwise it would just keep getting worse and I would start crying and not stop. I would do this same thing later on, after He took me. Only of course what I did, and what I felt, I felt, and did, much differently.

There were people walking in one direction and there were people walking in the other direction, so I moved away and I backed against this metal gate locked down in front of an empty storefront and I looked. I listened.

There were a lot of people and more things in my field of vision than I could process. By which I mean take in. Quiet music came through speakers somewhere in the ceiling, the sort of song the shopping center played when the time of year was something not like Christmas. A lot of people walked past and I heard parts of what they were saying and it had nothing to do with me.

I listened more than I looked but there was no sound of my mom's voice. I could not hear anybody calling my name, and while I knew she was, which is to say I just knew she must be, I could not hear her, or anyone else, looking for me. I knew that no matter what happened my mom was going to blame me. That I was going to get into trouble and that she was going to get mad even though I didn't do anything. I had just been walking. Same as her. I was definitely nervous. Even now I remember the feeling. But I also knew there was no point in just standing around, lost. Or, as I thought of it, not found. I knew that if I found her fast enough she might not have had time to realize that I had gone missing. Like if she had been looking at a pretty dress or at something for my dad or something. Anything.


I do not really remember this story fully. This is because now, which is to say since I killed Him and came home, this story is never spoken about. This is because this story, the one I am talking about inside this much bigger story, well this happened and then it was not much later that He stole me. By which I mean we are talking weeks. As in like less than my name's, which is to say a month's worth of days. And so any Ha Ha Remember Me stories, which would include the Remember Me Going Missing stories, or me in any other way doing something memorable stories, which ordinarily in most families would become one of the Do You Remember When? stories, well these, by which I mean those, are just not a part of our lives. He took those, too.

To certain thoughts, by which I mean memories, I have what psychiatrists call an animalistic purchase. They say, by which I mean write down, that I summon judgments concerning command without knowing what I'm doing. I have read this. I have looked at various reports and notes whenever I get the opportunity, which is more often than you would think. This is because they, by which I mean the doctors and the psychiatrists, think that I don't think, by which I mean care, about myself. This includes the past, present, and right now, by which I mean this is something that, if they happen to be thinking about me right now, they are thinking. I know what they mean. They mean that I make decisions without consideration. They say that I operate from a carefully cultivated certainty. I do not know about all that. What I do I do because it is right. I do not suffer from doubt.

Anyways, what I do remember is this. About being lost, I mean. And The Bee. And you do not, of course, have to believe me. Either what we remember is right, by which I mean accurate, or the opposite, by which I mean what we remember is false. There is no in-between. What is important to remember is that what you remember of any one event, by which I mean incident, is not, say, set in stone. It is as impermanent as the moment itself. And so our memories become memories of themselves. Over all of this we have no control. I will probably talk more about this later on. About the power, by which I mean importance, of memory. I say probably not because I worry I will forget, but because I have control over what I will, and will not say, and, right now, I am not sure.

My mother did not believe in hitting. So I must have been gone for a while. By then I was talking to this really nice girl who worked at this kiosk selling mechanical Bees. I was thinking my mom might want to get one for my dad because it was like a drone with a camera, and for a person who was not really into anything other than me and my mom he was, by which I mean at least sort of, into those kinds of things.

I do remember the Bee because this was one thing I did sometimes think about when He had me. By that I mean the times when He laid His hands on me. I remember how that Bee looked even more real than bees I saw outside, buzzing past or crawling around on flowers, which I know is a strange thing. This was because I was scared of bees, so I never saw one up super close. So I came to think of this Bee as the real thing.

The girl standing at the kiosk selling the Bee was nice and pretty, and because by then I was crying so hard and could not stop she said she would show me how it worked. What she was doing was to help calm me while I didn't hear my mom's name called over the speakers, breaking apart the non-Christmas music. It worked. I became a different sort of lost.

I remember that box, by which I mean the box the Bee came in. I remember that box like little else. I remember this one mother. She was there with her son. The mother was rude and all stressed out. The girl just shrugged. She looked at me and smiled. She crouched and nodded, by which I knew she wanted me to look closer. I did. She opened this locked cabinet. Inside the cabinet, which was down by her feet, was a small, wooden, box.

The box was about the size of a Magic 8 Ball, only of course it was a box, so it was not a circle. There was something, by which I mean a picture, on each side of the box. On the side of the box were images of a honey bee getting pollen from pretty flowers. A different type of flower on each side. A girl on the box wore this long sleeved dress, what I now know is a pinafore, a bonnet, and ankle boots. The girl was smooth like a stone and was beautiful. When thought about, by which I mean really looked at, and from different angles, the girl glittered in all these pretty colors. The girl made more of an impression than colors I could name. Hands cupped, arms outstretched, she rose like a sprite, only the toes of one foot on the ground.

The girl working the kiosk opened the box. Inside the box was a Bee. The Bee was pretty creepy. Disturbing. Actually, if I am being honest, and, honestly, why would there be a reason for me not to be, the sensation, by which I mean what I felt, was something closer to confusion. Like when you take a sip from a can and think it tastes red, but you discover it is actually green.

I remember that the mother, the girl's customer, asked a question. And I remember how the woman looked down on her child. The nice girl shrugged and took her phone and opened an application, closed another, and then set her phone to the side. The woman looked from the girl to her phone, to the Bee, and then to her child. The girl shrugged again, and then nodded. She reached for her phone and pushed a button. None of that is particularly important. But what is important is that you see my memory. That you understand it is still working.

The Bee flapped its wings and then its wings started fluttering so fast they became invisible. You only knew they were there because they were buzzing. I mean this was so loud you could hear the buzz over everything else going on around me. And then, like that, the Bee was off.

The Bee rose high into the air, buzzing first around my head before zipping and zagging into and out from a lot of shops. The Bee flew back closer before rising basically sort of straight up but to the side just a bit like a balloon. You are probably saying there is no way I remember something like this, but remember, it's not like I'm forty or something. This really did not happen all that long ago, by which I mean relatively speaking, and this was basically the only memory I played with when He still had me. It was not like I could push everything from my brain and memory, and so it was like a nice surprise when I found, which is to say thought of, something worth remembering. By which I mean something that wouldn't bother me, that wouldn't make things worse.

So the Bee, which was way up in one of those window features dotting the top of the food court, those thick glass constructions that rise from the ceiling like bubbles stuck to the ends of wands, hovered.

And the girl said, Watch. She told me to look at what happened. She pressed a button on her phone which worked as a remote control. What it does, she told me, is that it, by which she meant the Bee, creates this rad, psychedelic, sunbeam sort of shimmer, the vibration of its wings, or something, pooling the air to collect all of the colors it lets off. You see?

I did not understand the words coming out of her mouth. But I did understand, by which I mean I saw, what she meant.

And then the Bee fell. It was like this rope of color, like Hawaiian Punch poured from a pitcher, and the Bee, as if swatted dead, dropped. I remember that I gasped. And that the girl smiled. The Bee didn't hit the ground but, at the last possible moment, swooped up and flew over towards this other part of the food court. It landed on a table.

Because we, as people, are not prepared to be amazed, because everything we go through we already sort of know is coming, and we can thank the Internet for this, which is, by which I mean the Internet, basically just turning on and logging into life's commercial, the people in the shopping center either walked on by or, if they were sitting, stared at what they were planning on putting into their mouths. I mean, they didn't even see the beautiful Bee. How it was glowing purple and green, sort of blinking brighter and darker like Christmas lights on a Christmas tree. All that wonderful color from its little jellybean body striped black and yellow.

The girl pressed a couple of buttons and then turned her phone longwise and she held her phone like a remote control and she moved either side up or then down and then away and then towards her and the Bee crawled across a table, but slowly. Like a real bee the Bee stopped by a tipped cup and looked at the puddle from whatever spilled and was there on top of the table all sticky and smelling sweet like nectar. This one woman basically screamed and grabbed her tray and almost fell over. She was in such a hurry to leave her seat. By now of course I was not crying, I was laughing. A man in a suit saw the Bee and then looked all over the food court for somewhere else to sit. His face. It looked like he was smelling something really bad. It was amazing they, by which I mean everyone who saw the Bee, did not know they were scared of, or at least bothered by, something make-believe. I remember a lot more, but there are these two most important things.

The first is this: The Bee stopped to check the spill. When the Bee stopped moving, it turned back into its basic color. I remember this because this is one of the best thoughts I have ever thought, and I am talking about ever, and not just because I was little. This is what I thought.

Light seemed to come out from inside the Bee, and this made a little shadow. The Bee when it did not move got so bright it seemed like it was getting warm, like someone set it on fire. The color grew so bright that my mind sort of went blank and I wondered what came first, thoughts, or the words that made the thoughts. If we did not think in words, I thought then, and thought about all the time when He had me, would we think in pictures? I thought about this over and over again and again when He had me, and there was so much time and just that one book He did not take away to use up my imagination. I am still not sure, and of course I never will be, but I will never stop thinking about this, and I know I will one day come up with an opinion. And I will get to the book, as well. By which I mean I will get around to telling you about it, I mean. That, and that it is pretty interesting how it really is a fact that no one philosopher has ever come up with an original idea. Other than the very first one. Who is a person we don't know. Which is the reason why Plato and which is the reason why Socrates is so famous. Thoughts are there to be made. They just happened to be there to make them. More than that, they were in position to record them, by which I mean write down what I'm sure were thoughts previously considered.

The second important thing I remember is the way my mom squirmed her way through people walking in the other direction. How just like a broken Bee she flew through the mall. How, when I first realized I was seeing her, she, just like any other rude person, brushed and bumped against other people. I should have thought she was scared and angry, but I forgot I was missing and that as far as she knew I was lost and that maybe something terrible had happened to me and so I was smiling, very happy and waving like wild, bursting to tell her about the girl and the Bee. She, by which I mean my mom, was not exactly like Him, but she was, sort of, by which I mean in the way I soon saw, and fast, that something was really, really wrong. Which by that I mean she was not in control. That she didn't see me. That she was seeing what she thought had happened to me and had not yet erased that from what she was seeing and I stepped towards her as she stepped almost running towards me and with her arm back and her palm open she smacked me so hard I didn't even have time to understand. To see. I saw white. I fell to the ground. My whole head stung. I heard a little bit of everything.

And so when my mom saw those pictures of me on TV and she understood that someone sold pictures of me from before I was stolen she was crying. Even my dad might have been crying, too. And I have never seen him cry. And I understand why. For them, those pictures were my Bee.

By the time I won my pine cone game my hair went past my shoulders and was sort of spiraling. Even though I cut my hair, that part the producers and the writers did get more yes than less right, I can still feel it sometimes when I wake up after falling asleep. Especially when I wake up after having fallen asleep without planning to.

Anyways. Once I did go ten for ten I considered that one game over. Next, I started throwing pinecones at the pinecones I had already thrown, the idea being to try and knock them to the ground. This is not as easy as I'm sure some of you are saying it seems. Plus, like I said, I only played when I knew He was not at home. That, and it didn't rain all that often. And when it did rain it would stay rainy for a long period of time which meant it did not matter, I was staying inside until He knew it was going to stop. So I didn't get to practice as much as I would have liked. Once I went ten for ten I was going to consider that game over as well. But I killed Him before it got to that.


At first, back before I needed to brush and cut my hair, I would start drying the rain by drying everything using dry towels. He always gave me twenty, and the nice kind, too, like you get at expensive hotels. This, the towel part, is why detectives thought, at least for a little while, that He worked in a hotel. That He was involved in travel and tourism.

Anyways, the towels were thick. Heavy. I of course used them on the grass as well. By this I mean I set a certain number of dry towels to this one side. But once I used them they got so soaking wet and so very fast that I never dried the rain. Because this was in the beginning, and hitting me was still new for Him, and I guess for whatever reason kind of fun, or part of His lesson planning, so I, since I didn't want to get hit, came up with a plan.

My plan was this: What I did was that I thought to use the other, soaking wet towels, first. I would get the van and the patio chairs dry, and I would do that using as few towels as possible. And then, after wringing those towels as dry as imaginable, I would use them first. By which I mean to dry the grass. I was proud of myself. I was maybe only eight. Or whatever. It doesn't really matter. Still. It just was not right. It did not work. No matter how long I spent outside, and no matter how bright the sun was shining, and even when the wind was blowing the grass, and even after I used the damp, wrung out towels and then used the totally·dry towels, the grass was still soaking wet when He came out to check. He was not particularly happy. Which is something you know because this right here is an example of something the producers and the writers do get right.

.   .   .

I am not sure how I know I am pretty, I just know that I am. This is nothing I debate, or even consider. About everything I try never to wonder.

Yeah, right, I hear some of you mutter.

Sure, Mallory, I read many of you typing.

If you were me, and no matter what you feel or what you think after watching *Dry The Rain*, which makes me, because I killed Him more than because I survived, a mankiller more than a survivor, there is nothing cool or fun about being me. Trust me. But that to the side. If you were me, you wouldn't either. Wonder, I mean. When mornings and afternoons and evenings and nights are erased and all there is is lightness and darkness, something like going around wondering about anything is, you come to find, a bad thing. But I cannot help wondering about one thing and that would be this: I do wonder if not so pretty people, and by this I do not mean all not so pretty people, really, but not so pretty girls my age, I wonder if they, themselves, would not think they were not so pretty if it were not for other people. Or, I wonder, would they, like me, simply know how they seemed? I guess what I'm asking is if ugliness is a thing.


While I do not think this is the same thing, or fair or good, it is true, and to be clear I'm not talking about people like Him, people who have been disfigured and so because their faces are scarred, or marred, or whatever, that being this totally and other discussion, by which I mean that should be obvious, when it comes to how everyone looks, by which I mean basically, it is just as obvious that not everyone can be pretty. Otherwise, no one could be not so pretty. That is just how this world works. The way we set things up, there is no middle. There is good and there is bad. There is strong and there is weak. There is your finger, and there is your fingernail. There is nothing, and there is something. And while life would be so much better if we just let things be, we do not. The world works this certain way. But the way of the world does not have to work this way. We do not have to judge one another based on how we look. But I do this myself. So, then, ugliness must be true? Or maybe not. Maybe prettiness is what is true. And prettiness, at least when it comes to girls and to women as it is declared by men, and to be honest not even men but by something inside of them, and if you believe in God, well, then, yes, it would have been placed there by God, and so prettiness is a thing. But only because we make it so, is what I mean. If God made us and I, just to say me, personally, know that he did, and if we have fallen, which, by which I mean us, know that we have, a great question is not what this says about us, but what this says about God.

But imagine that you think I am pretty or are attracted to me and of course most of you do and are, and by that I mean either from the age I was in those photos they show in the introduction, the pictures captured of me and posted online, or of the other me, by which I mean Mallory. But what if *Dry The Rain* starring Fill In The Name was made not because I was pretty, but because of how great I played Tic-Tac-Toe. Or how great I was at shoelace tying. You know what I mean. Which is to say you could, if you wanted to. Some of you say that I am crazy, but I know what I am talking about. What is up to you is if you want to figure this out.

I will try and help. Think this. Not so pretty girls would not have to think they were pretty, but anything would be better than knowing you were not that pretty. Especially if you get stolen. After not so pretty girls are stolen and hurt I would bet my life most of those girls do not make it longer than a few days and maybe even hours, depending. There is always someone prettier out there to steal and this being a mostly easy thing to do, too, for men like Him. Because, and while I am sure of this, by which I mean they, by which I mean men like Him, obviously do not want to get caught, they are not afraid of getting caught. Obviously they are cautious, that goes without saying, but that is not what I mean. They do not care. They are just not worried. They do not think that far ahead because they only worry about this one thing. Which is girls like me. And how much fun it is, by which I mean thrilling, to hunt us. Or how some of them just can't stop. Which is another story. One not worth getting into. Anyways, one thing even we can all agree on is that none of them get made into their own TV shows. These not as pretty and stolen girls, that is to say. And there is definitely something to think about there, when you stop and think about it.

For obvious reasons I didn't have a mirror, but, as a prisoner, once you are taken and stolen, and especially after a very long time, you get good at finding ways to look at yourself, and you get good at ways of looking at yourself. Which of course are two different things. And I am just being honest and I am only saying this to make a point, by which I mean when I saw my face I saw that I was pretty, and even though I was little I knew that this mattered. Or one thing I will repeat is this. It helped.

This, and how I grew to get these nice big boobs I now have and how they became these parts of me He would often play with and enjoy. As if my breasts were to Him this wonderful mystery. He was more surprised than me. He was happy. I know this because He was obviously not unhappy.

And because it was exactly around this time when He started to feed me much differently. By which I mean way different than before.

Before, what was really different was that He did not care what He gave me. Because He didn't want me to die, by which I mean by accident, and because He didn't want me to get sick, and then have to kill me, Him taking me to the doctor not being this option, while I wouldn't say He gave me good, or healthy things, He fed me regularly. This was food that I imagined He made for Himself, and then made extra, since He was already busy cooking. So a lot of eggs and bacon. These gross, what I now know are liverwurst sandwiches. And for dinner food like spaghetti and sausage. And all sorts of microwave dinners. And once a week, which I now think were Fridays, pepperoni, always pepperoni, pizza.

What was different, by which I mean when my body started to change, was that He started giving me these really gross and thick white, brown, and pink shakes. I think they were supposed to taste like vanilla, chocolate, and strawberry, but they tasted like straw and dirt. But one thing I can tell you is that they worked. They filled me up. And I would feel more up than filled and even though I was doing this before, I started to what you would call work out, and I did this for a few different reasons. Pretty soon in time I built, both He and I were surprised to find, this really nice and really strong body. What some of you all might call totally tight and perfectly fit. Imogen Appleton talks about this.

What I did, and what Imogen Appleton talked about, and still does, when asked, was I exercised in the cellar. This was because I knew there would come a time when He got old enough and I would need to be strong enough and I would need to be ready to kill Him. By which, to repeat myself because I really want to get this point across, I of course mean strong enough. This is something *Dry The Rain's* producers and the writers just can't get right. What was going on in and through my mind. And not just when it comes to me getting strong, but anything. Not even close. But the really and truly important thing to remember is that they do not care. So why should I? Or why should you? By which I mean care. But that is a question like asking a child, Why is the sky blue?


Even from the beginning, not from that first day He stole me but the first day the shock and fear wore off and I began to not so much want to live as I was afraid of dying. Whenever that was. From that point and then forever on I knew that He was dying. This was because I knew death. Right before He stole and took me, my dad's mom died, by which I mean my grandma. Many of you probably do not believe I knew He was dying, and not that I need to, but this is the only way I can explain how I knew. By which I mean like this.

When you are around death you get this certain sort of feeling for it. Which of course is not the same as what people say when they say they get a taste for something. If you try, you will see. And of course His cellar. Like how when you scream in a cave or a tunnel, and what that sounds like makes you aware of where you are as much as any other sensation, this, which is to say His cellar, where you are as much as any other sensation, this, which is to say His cellar, felt like death in many weird and understandable ways.

Anyways. My parents were not that close with my dad's family. They were much older because my dad's mom, my grandma who I really loved, had him by accident when she was almost fifty. I guess she was not quite old enough to get that much attention for being that old and having a baby. I mean she was not ninety, and I suppose that even back then older women having babies was not this rare of a thing. Back then, like now, which is what I call not the Information but the Icon Age, it was not that a lot of stuff did not mean anything any longer, it was just that this was the start of everybody making sure their stuff meant something, or seemed important, and people did not want to connect, people did not worry about missing out on things. Well they still worried, but in different ways. By which I mean people could choose how to worry. People could choose what to miss. And then what they would do is this: Talk about it. And since there was so much to choose and so much to miss, people, well, they might have evolved, by which I mean they got what I say was worried and upset way less. So yeah. No. Things were much different. And I am fine if that does not make sense. It does, but you simply have to think in a different way.

Sayings, by which I mean aphorisms, well these were taken over by letters, which is to say letter by letter, by which I mean acronyms. That, and people fell under spells, by which I mean other people's dreams, way too easily. No one doubted anything, or, to be more precise, no one cared and no one wanted to use the energy to do so. Those people who did still care and called out cynicism, by which I mean this particular sort of caring, or not caring, were gone. Do not take my word for it. Just put my name in Google with the word .gif or meme and of course you will find what I mean. Or how it is when during a football game a player is maybe paralyzed. Or that one time when that player while he was tackling another player suffered this heart attack and almost died. People around him, by which I mean his friends and teammates, and other players on the field or those people in the stands, knew there was a chance they were going to be on TV, and it was so obvious that they wanted to look as though what was happening to the player was somehow happening to them. I am sure you do not know what I mean. But that is okay by me, too. It is possible, though. By which I mean to know. Just so you know.

But around where she and where my mom lived my dad's birth and her pregnancy was definitely pretty big news, the story being printed in *The Standard*, her picture put right there above what you would call the fold. My parents, which really is to say my mom, still have the clipping. My grandma in a white hospital gown and her black and gray hair, what you would call salt and pepper, pulled into a ponytail that was falling apart. She looks tired but happy cradling her child, my dad, against her chest. He looks so tiny and pink, all but wrapped up in this tiny knitted hat.

After a while my grandparents moved to live way up in Maine. I'm not sure why. I do remember that my grandpa died, by which I mean I have this vague impression, an idea that was made more real by the fact that for so much of my life he was not around. He was not this person I ever saw. There being nothing to miss, I was not sad. If anything, I was happy to have so much of my grandma just for me. Then she got sick. So unless we visited her, I did not see her. She was a prisoner that way.

My last memory of my grandmother, by which I mean before she came to move in with us, is not a good one. We were at the table and dinner was over. It was awful and boring being up there, by which I mean her house in Maine, but it was really fun going outside. I waited and waited to be let go so I could get out and play in the woods before it got too dark and my parents made me come inside. This was more because they were worried about wild animals than me getting stolen by men like Him. And even that is kind of what you would call romantic. Wild animals were pretty much dead things even back then. Which, again, in case you forgot or were not paying attention, was not that long ago. What it is is that I am sure they were worried about me getting lost.

When I was finally free from sitting at the table not eating dinner I was so happy to be excused that I pushed back from my plate and swung from my chair and I banged and smashed right into my grandma. With my left elbow I hit her right in one of those spots where she hurt the worst, directly where they were radiating her, and even though she did not eat much she puked what food she had eaten down the front of her shirt. None of the food was digested, so what was there looked exactly like the food on her plate. But she could not stop needing to puke.

She was my favorite person ever, and every once in a while when He had me I could not help but think of her. Another thought I am still proud of is that even though of course I wanted her alive, that does go without saying, well if she was going to die I am glad she died before He got a hold of and stole me. This is because it, my being stolen, would have been worse for her than even my mom. Well, if not worse, close. Or worse, in a different way. And not just because of how much she loved me, but because of how much she loved my mom, her daughter, as well. She would have to deal with worrying about me and her own daughter at the same time, and that is just too much worrying for any mother. That, more than any cancer, would have killed her.

. . .

My grandma lived with us when she could no longer live on her own and so I have lots of memories. By which I mean of her. But we saw her all of the time before then and so I have lots of other memories, too. I will not write about any of them because I do not want to in any way change them, by which I mean how I remember her, which is something that will happen. That, and too much stuff about my grandparents, and even my parents, just is not the point. You'll just have to believe me, because some things I really do know.


With Him it was kind of like that, by which I mean the sound of His breathing, although of course I disliked the sound for different reasons completely. Listening to Him breathe was like hearing my grandma that one dinner, by which I mean how after puking she breathed, by which I mean wheezed, and how each wheeze was a terrible sounding thing. From very early on. From almost, which is to say from just about the beginning of being stolen, and of course by this I mean after I got used to the idea of being taken, I knew I was going to need to wait a long time. Relatively speaking. By which I mean I just knew He was going to keep me around because otherwise why was I still around? And that meant if I was just calm He was soon going to be gone. That gave me my problem. The problem was that, until Mary, I could not think of a solution.

Some of you think I am an idiot and that is because you insist none of this, by which I mean none of what happened to me could ever be considered lucky. But again, you are exactly wrong. If I am lucky at all, I am lucky in that way. One of the worst things about Him taking me was the idea that I had some sort of choice. No matter what happened, that part of it all, the idea that I had a choice in anything, that was just what was so tiring and, in time, became that from which I most wanted to be free. Ways. Choices. Options. Decisions. I of course did not want it to be by Him, but I wanted taking care of. I did not want to have to think. You would or might maybe understand if you were or have ever been anything other than free. And by this I mean truly.

His hair was already white when He stole me, and He was definitely strong, but strong in the way overweight and unhealthy people are strong. By which I mean for just a little bit at a time. This, and how they are kind of wild and unable to control their energy. How they can really and truly hurt you both if they want to and when they don't mean to. He breathed as though there was something caught in His throat. The sound was absolutely gross and totally disgusting. He was so not healthy. And of course He smoked those cigarettes as well. A lot of cigarettes. And to point out a fact, I never saw Him without smoke coming from His face. I mean relatively speaking. Aside from that morning when He was smiling and standing by His van, I have never seen Him without a cigarette. He was smart in those ways.

There was a sink in the cellar, and I was expected to brush my teeth. And to floss as well. Not that I would not, which is to say I didn't need the lesson He gave me, the one you see in Episode Two, that so dumb and idiotic *Fight or Flight*, where He uses the food coloring and the deck of playing cards, but you would not probably think this is something He would make me do. But while He was not many things, He was many things. And He knew that if He wanted to keep me around He needed me healthy in every possible way, and it is not like He could take me to the dentist. What is more than this, I was prettier and of course smelled better and was what you might call groomed.

If you have ever been to a museum and held a chain that slaves, which I know should be called enslaved persons, though I'm not sure I fully agree, but anyways, this isn't about me, by which I mean not really, as in quite actually, so if you have ever been at a museum and have ever held a chain that slaves were chained in, you have felt just how heavy chains can be. And here I am talking about the chains that were screwed into His wall that led to the parts He put around my foot. Or feet you could say, depending. I am not comparing myself to anyone, but I am saying that this object, my chain, or chains, was, or were, heavy.

One day, when there was no rain for weeks, and my ankle ached from the chain, I definitely and for sure had had it. Which by that I mean enough. With my chain, they, by which I mean the producers and the writers, they do get most of this exactly right. Which by that I mean that what you see is what I got. I mean, they, the producers and the writers, they would literally have to not get it right on purpose because of course they owned my chains. And with all of that for them to pick up, look at, consider, and talk about, there was also me. By which I mean I was obligated to answer questions. And when it came to my chains I told them the truth about it all, I answered all of their questions and I even gave them more stuff they did not think to ask, by which I mean things that had been, were, could, or might be important. Mostly. But that was only because this was an easy way of me looking like I was doing what I agreed to do.

I even got sort of smart, or you could say clever, and I pretended it was something that I did not want to talk about, and you could just see them, by which I mean the producers and the writers, get so excited, and how their eyes and minds worked to figure out ways, they thought, to trick me. By which I mean to keep on going. To keep on talking. About my chains. So that was funny. But my point is that to get any of that wrong, by which I mean the information about my chain, they, the producers and the writers, they would have be confident that their writers making something up and showing that, by which I mean filming something that was not true, was either more realistic or was going to be more interesting to you. While I do not particularly care, I have seen enough to say that it looks like they got it mostly right. If anything, they went underboard. They showed me chained up, by which I mean not chained up, less that I actually was. Because remember, I wasn't chained up constantly.

But when it came to stuff regarding the chains as chains, that part does look right. There was no shackle. If I am going to be literal, it was a dog's choke chain He fastened around my foot. The chain was heavy and metal and smooth and cool and thick and round. Some people, by which I mean FBI experts, say He made His chains. By which I mean He somehow ordered them. While I do not particularly care, this could be true. I can see how this matters. By which I mean I see how this would interest you. All that I know is this. Each small metal oval, by which I mean link, there were twenty-two of them, was locked to the other. I could sort of slide the metal up and down maybe less than just part of what I consider an inch. I could twist a metal ring, by which I mean one of them, individually, but only one, and I could only twist a little bit before the others closest to it on either side of the chain tightened and pinched. If I moved a certain way it would get tighter, and the chain would get even tighter when I tried to loosen it, and while that hurt what after a while hurt the most was just always having something rubbing my skin. Even if it did not hurt in a way that you might recognize, it was just the alwaysness of it that in my mind turned those chains into pain. I in no way can say this for sure, but it is my best guess that yes, He invented and made those things, because there was one for each leg, just for me. Just for us girls.

You might think that you are the only person to think that using my bar of soap and water would help, and you ask your friends why didn't I, or you tell each other you cannot believe I didn't. By which I mean use warm water and the bar of soap. I cannot tell you the number of things I did and did not do, and the number of things that I did and did not do that the writers and the producers for whatever their reasons just do not show you, and if you want to just believe what they show you or, for whatever your reasons, pick your spots and choose what not to believe, that is not on me. That is on you. And on top of all of that, many of the things I told them that they, by which I mean the producers and the writers do use, by which I mean incorporate as parts of *Dry The Rain*, they, for whatever their producer and writer reasons, use differently. And by differently I do not necessarily mean intentionally, because remember, the producers and the writers are just people, who, as I may have said before, know not what they do.


Anyways, this once, when I was chained up and just had enough, I considered eating my tube of toothpaste. I just went through what was left in the cellar, a really old and crusty tube of Crest. What, of course, the girls before me used. He replaced this with a big tube of Crest that did not last as long as you would think, because brushing my teeth was something to do and was something that tasted different after He taught me something or did something, and so I brushed my teeth a lot. And these were just some of the reasons I brushed my teeth four times a day. Or sometimes even more.

Before He stole me and used things like eggshells and pencil shavings to teach me things, my mom, when it came to toothpaste, always made sure I only applied a pea-sized amount upon my brush and would get really nervous and quite upset if I swallowed any, by which I mean I sometimes did, because I thought it tasted really good and so I would swallow it, this of course being the kind for little kids that tastes like candy.

Poison, she would yell. Spit it out, Spit it out.

And then I would have to rinse my mouth out.

So it made sense that toothpaste was poisonous and that it would kill me. But I could not take more than one bite. I just could not do this. Eating toothpaste was so disgusting and gross that I just spit it out. I chose to live. That, or I just was not up for feeling sick or, more exactly, was not quite able to make myself be so. And so yes. If you want to know the truth, and many of you only say that you do, no matter what you see on *Dry The Rain*, this is it. Eating a big bite of toothpaste was my one and only attempt to kill myself.

I had not had my period yet. He did not want to hurt parts of me, or do something to parts of me, that would get all of that going or, if not that, He was afraid of doing something that might make me need a doctor. It is not like He could have me all sick and infected and rotting. Stinking, to be quite crass and direct. Which would mean He would have to kill me. I said I was careful. I said He was careful. I never said He was intelligent.

He did not want to make me look not so pretty. All He wanted was to stick different parts of His body into different parts of mine. But for Him I was this perfect dream. I have not read about men like Him, but I could write a book about men like Him because not only were we together for a long time, He was the only person I was around for a long time. You get to know a guy this way. And it doesn't matter who he is. And so what happened to me was this.

Once I killed Him and figured out, by which I mean I was told by Mary, how to get away, I was pretty quickly put back together with my parents. This was not quite as fast as you would think, though. As in like a matter of hours. Or even days. But that is another story. I was never told exactly the reason why. By which I mean why we were not put back together immediately. I am sure many of you have an idea, or that of course you say you know. Fine. The point of this being that there was time.

Something that I did and something that I now still do was think of Him. By that I mean I thought other people were so different because of the ways they did things, which were in no way at all like how He did things. How all of them, by which I mean you, had so many ways of doing different things the same way. As in, far more yes than less. How it was that He did things so much differently was just so obvious to me. I did not have to look or think about this.

The, by which I mean His differences, were just so obvious. And they were all so different from your way. Which is not so unique, or different, as you think or often say. There is only one time I ever talk about this, by which I mean there is really only one thing to say. And that is this.

Sometimes when little kids go missing, and even more when, however rare, little kids who have gone missing are found, these certain people from the FBI call me. They ask my mom and they ask my dad if it is okay if they ask me a couple of questions. I know you know all about missing kids and what to say about unsubs from your watching that one serial killer TV show, and that you equally know what to say about serial killers and how they operate from your listening to that one podcast, *Killing Me Softly*. Well, because that is a show I do not watch, and because that is a podcast I do not hear, it is sort of like comedy. I can't say that they get everything wrong, but I can say that so much of what you think they get right is completely made up, by which I mean the stuff of producers and writers, and that right there is what I find funny.


The podcast is sort of funny in a different way, too, by which I mean sad. This is because the hosts are the sorts of drug addicts who no longer do drugs but who lost their careers because they did so many drugs and so they came up with making other people's misery entertaining and funny as a way to make not only lots of money but names for themselves again. How redeeming. But the TV show. This is the worst. How they, by which I mean the writers, go and make the characters have relationships, the characters on that TV show, it's like they all go to the same church or something and hang out together after work talking about their divorces and personal demons. So stupid. So dumb. I know, I know. I just said I don't watch the show. That I don't listen to the podcast. But, unlike many of you, I truly pay attention. There being many more ways than one to learn.

But that to the side. There is not even a Behavioral Analysis Unit. A BAU. By which I mean in the FBI. Which is something many of you believe is this real and true thing from watching TV. And you are pointing and screaming in a manner of speaking and saying how would I know if I do not go online and also that I am wrong, that there are criminal psychologists. And once again you are right, there are criminal psychologists. But have you thought about this? Say there was a new episode of that one serial killer show on TV every Tuesday night every single week of every single year. For more than twelve years. That would mean that there are, if you do not take into account the different cliffhanger episodes, and I will not, that means that, at least, there are fifty-two serial killers, and really twisted and creative serial killers at that, all sorts of tormented men with genius IQs killing people every year like Einstein solved equations.

Or go and times that number by twelve. Or whatever.

That is what makes the show so funny. The idea that there are so many serial killers. That, and the fact that the producers have the writers go so far away from what is real so that each and every serial killer is as wild and fun as Willy Wonka. Well, in a manner of me speaking.

The podcast women are just as bad. Worse, really. This is because they, these podcast women, unlike the writers, who, after all, are just writers laughing in their draft room tombs, take themselves seriously. This is because they go back and dig up these terrible stories that families just want forgotten and go about laughing and paying only people like themselves all while saying Fuck as if every time they say fuck they get an extra ten dollar bonus, which of course because ten dollars by itself is not that much money means they have to say fuck a lot, and here I mean a super number of times if they want to make saying fuck add up to an amount of money that matters. Which of course they do. So there is that, too.

They have fans, these podcasters, and they make people fans of serial killers. Could you imagine having, by which I mean spending time from your life thinking about and then selecting and choosing and then having, which is to say in your life, a favorite person who used, say, hot tin foil and a can opener to cut people open before killing them? It's like the podcasters are professors and their fans are coeds majoring in sadism. Do not get me wrong. This does not make you, should you be such a student, a serial killer or a pedophile, and this does not make you as bad as a serial killer or a pedophile. But I am asking: What does this make you?

And I am not saying there are copycats, pedophiles and killers who, like school shooters, go on to steal and take and rape and kill little girls because of shows like *Dry The Rain*. What I am saying, though, is that admiring or glorifying these mostly men is hideous. That it's a particular sort of evil. And to go out of your way, and I mean really out of your way, to find never before discussed women serial killers as a means to add popular content? Well, you get the idea.

You probably, and just now, went to Google and with your keywords googled and found what you wanted to find and of course there being something that you wanted to find you probably went, See! The FBI thinks there are twenty-five or maybe fifty serial killers in the United States alone. But see what happens at the end of every episode of that one partic-ular show is that the serial killer is either caught or dies. So serial killers are even more rare than an endangered species.

Than dinosaurs. And then the women and their podcast shows. They have to go digging for stories because there are just not that many that interest you or that could possibly introduce you to one of the possibles for your favorite serial killer because there are just not that many. As in that many with what they, and so you, consider interesting stories. You just must think. That FBI number, which, I must say, is a guess, is crazy, but they are not saying there are that many new serial killers born or making their first kill each year. Many of those guys have been around forever.

So? I hear you texting.

Really? I see you posting.

If that is so true.

If I am so right.

Why, then, you wonder, does the FBI call me?

Well, this is actually a pretty interesting story, but to make the long part of this short, this is because it takes a really long time to catch one of these people, if ever, and so many of their, by which I mean the FBI's questions, are about the same people. Or someone who might be the same person. At least that is what I would say if you asked me. And they, the FBI people, what they do is they think if they keep putting information together, and if they keep asking the same questions about different cases, or different questions about the same cases, they might, even if nothing else, get something like an idea. What you would call a lead. But, for the most part, most of those cases are just cold, cold, cold, cold, cold.


To Him, I was special. Just imagine. You have this thing for little girls where what you do to them and what you teach them makes you feel great. And then on top of being pretty, I was tall. So already I was almost like a teen. So for all the time He had me I was basically a little girl with this teenager's body. He has basically got like this mythological creature. But here is the creepy part, and it takes a lot to make me think once, let alone twice. But all the while He has me He has in this famous Imogen Appleton another little growing girl that he can look at in the movies and look at on TV and flip through in magazines and click on His computer to look at and study. So creepy. So think about it. What are you doing when you are watching *Dry The Rain*? Anyways, so much of this protected me.

What this? you say.

To which I say, You will just have to trust that I know what I mean.

A big for example, or maybe an exception to this, and by that I mean me being protected, is that when mad, which is to say when He got angry, He was pretty careful with a pipe or an iron to hit my shoulders and my legs. With a pipe or an iron. Which by iron I mean yeah, the sort you use on clothing. And by pipe I mean something you would use for part of your plumbing. This is to say that He was still hitting my body. This is to say that He was still hurting me. There was definitely something that He definitely did get out of hitting me, and I am not saying there wasn't. You could see this look that would cover His face and how, when He was done, the look on His face was as if His face had been covered in mud and then, once He was done, by which I mean hitting and teaching me, He had showered off and washed Himself clean. His face looked back at me differently. And of course getting hurt did hurt and was for sure scary, but it was nothing at all like the few times when He lost control and got me in the throat or in the ear or on the collar bone or the mouth or on my vagina.

. . .

Beatings could get out of His hands. I am not saying they did not. Once He punched out a baby tooth. Once, with His palm, He hit my forehead so hard that my eye started bleeding. Or, more likely, something inside me started bleeding, and that blood from whatever it was that was actually bleeding came out my eye. After that happened He turned around and went upstairs and He did not return for many days. He did not chain me. He left food, sometimes shakes, sometimes not, on the top step. He said, Food. He was scared He ruined me. And while I am happy for me, I do feel bad for the not so pretty ones, the ones who were not beautiful to Him because my point, which I was making before, is that He did not keep them, those other ones, by which I mean that He would rape and sodomize them and then get bored with their faces and their bodies and that He would move on, that hunting for Him was fun and that is why I think He was sick and dying because when He got me He planned on what you could call retiring. By which I mean He was hunting for someone who looked like me, a girl that, once found, He would keep.

This is something I do not think about too often, but He was going to kill me. Now of course many of you do not, but supposing you did believe my take on things, by which I mean my theories on Him, and how He was, and what He was doing, you, even though I do not, have an answer to this question. Well that is fine and good. DM me. Or, here, try this. Email. Get me at andyouarelookinglive@gmail.com. It is not as if there is a point in anonymity. It is not as though enough of you don't find some way to reach me. And to say stuff much less interesting. That you're sure has never before been said. But putting that to the side, while I knew He was sick, while He was dying was something I just knew to be true, there was no way to know if He was going to live for two or four years or maybe even more. So what, I thought, was a girl to do?

While I knew that I was His final girl, I knew there would come a time when I would become too much work. When He would no longer need me to dry the rain. And that idea was scary. Because of course when that time came, by which I mean when He retired, the gift He gave to Himself, which He was of course a long time planning, would be allowing Himself to kill me. Which, because I would be His last kill, by which I mean I was what many of you all would call a Final Girl, would be a particularly protracted, by which I mean inventive, death.

Final Girl.

Ah, well. While this is nothing I want to get into, and won't, by which I mean at least not really, I will say something, if only because so many of you already have, and do, and that something is this.

Many, if not most of you, by which of course I mean You, really do believe that you, because you, too, are so misunderstood and so very strong, want to be a Final Girl. That you, unlike your friends, would by some man in a mask avoid getting your throat slit, or your head hammered in, that you do not have to worry about getting shot but that you would avoid getting strangled, or drowned, by someone in your life who, because of something deeply personal, is going around killing other people in your life, up to and including family members, acquaintances, and friends. Pet dogs, even. Sure, you think, you might not technically be a virgin, but you are virginal, by which you know you are pure, and righteous, and good, and that this means you, somehow, more so than the others, not only don't deserve to die so much as you have the right to live. You, you know, are smart, tenacious, and brave, and that you, like me, would find a way to survive. Please. Forget me. I only ask you this: After thinking about all of the movies, and now all of the books, how many Final Girls have you read about in the news?

Anyways. When He knew that He was going to die, and that He was going to give Himself His present, I knew that this was going to be an incredible and demented moment. A moment so demented and incredible that this, by which I mean however He designed to kill me, would be impossible to show not just on TV, but even in the movies.

In the beginning I was very scared and was very worried about drying the rain. If it was not for the grass I could have gotten it, by which I mean drying the rain, all done. And I could have dried the rain pretty easily, but of course the grass was not the point of it all. Whatever that was. Which I now know. Which you think is impossible to ever understand and so why, then, do your answers, and why does this topic and #drytherain always trend, and then I remember why and that is because there is nothing that you do not know. That, and so many of you do not know how to have boredom. You will not allow boredom to interfere with your lives.

What I learned about grass drying was to start with a corner. I tried all four at different points in time, and I mixed this up depending on how wet it was outside, how much it had rained, and so on, but it really did not matter where I started, the ground was completely and totally level. The main and only point was starting with just one corner. And to then really and truly concentrate.

Barefoot, using your foot sideways, like a rake, or, in my case, a golf club, the small one, what you would call a putter, you rake the lawn in the same way. By which I mean direction. Really, really, take your time. It is not like there was ever this hurry. It was not like He ever said, You have four hours to dry the rain. There was all day, if I wanted.

In the beginning and when I was really scared is when I worked the most. When He was home I knew that He watched me. Sure, He took what I considered commercial breaks, but I learned, and this pretty much from the beginning, that what I was doing was His TV. Well, some of it was, anyways.

Now do not get me wrong. I am not contradicting. I am not taking anything back. He kept me because of my face. My body. But, and here you are right. Here you are correct. This is nothing I can prove. This is something I can only claim. But in terms of me being a TV show? In terms of Him watching me and being fascinated? The others did not give Him quite so much pleasure. But, to be fair, that is because they, unlike me, were not alive long enough to think things through. I, too, gave Him a bunch of reruns before offering up new, what you would call in this comparison, episodes. Or seasons.

When you are raking the grass with your foot, your other foot planted behind you so that with your rake you can really press down and deep into the Earth, water bubbles to the surface and squishes between your toes. You rake and you stop. You rake and you stop. And you drag your foot across and to the other end of the yard.

You are out of your chain and even after an hour and even after an afternoon you cannot possibly get used to the feeling which, if you could use only one would, I would choose lightness. And it is not because the chains are heavy, which of course they are, but more because when you are chained to a wall and only have this tiny area to move around in your body begins to sink in on itself and you begin to feel every little bit of yourself all added up to make this one great weight. Remember, if you have forgotten, I was so young when so much of this happened. So, other than the dictionary, I of course did not read. And because I was so little, by which I mean young, I had next to nothing by way of school, or experience, to go on. By which I mean help me. And so I did not have this understanding to have the words to say how I felt. And since that time it is only possible to remember how it felt to be feeling that way. By which I mean those are the only words, the few that I knew, that I have for something like this, and those would be words not worth typing out. And so even in typing this I am not getting it correct, I am only giving you this idea. But here. Try this.

If we are talking specifically about drying the grass carefully, you must be mindful to avoid retracing your steps because, like I have said, you don't want to make underwater water. So this means you then walk in a wide sort of circle, and you return to your original corner all the while trying to forget the soft silky grass and even when you catch between your toes one of the worms, how cool and surprising this feels. With your back sort of pressed against the fence, or wall, only this time standing about half a foot away from where you started, you repeat the process. Do this for hours and hours, making sure to keep in mind to make smaller circles. And you do this until you have raked the entire lawn, until you have squeezed yourself in this tiny corner that is on the opposite part of the yard from where you first started.

That being done and taken care of, now you get on your hands and knees and use the towels. It's almost impossible not to make some underwater water, so you do the best you can. First, use the damp towels that you have used to clear the patio furniture and His van, which, after drying those, you have squeezed out and left spread on the driveway to dry. But you must be super careful that there is no way a towel is going to get blown by the wind and, say, fall under His van so that you do not see it is lost. Of course you would not, but let us for the sake of imagination say you did. You will only make this mistake once.

Once you have done that, then you dry the rain using the dry towels. I can't say how many times I have dried the rain, or if I ever have, by which I mean as in really and actually. But as far as He was concerned?

I have.

My reward for drying the rain was that there was no punishment. This, and He started to check my work less.

He would not give me scissors to have, but He did make me cut my hair. He did not like short hair. With a curling iron this was something that He taught me after my first snip. But He did not like long hair, either. Like everything with Him, getting everything right took a bit of time. A couple of lessons. But, to be honest, He was very regular and He did not often change things up. He was deliberate and exact.

What He did was He made me take off my shirt. To use His words He ordered me topless.

Not as in, Take off your shirt.

No.

He would say, I order you topless.

For this there was no reason other than the obvious. Then He would go upstairs and come back downstairs with a pair of scissors in His back pocket. Then with a finger swollen and crooked, its long nail yellowed and thick and covered with oil, He placed the scissors, which were more yes than less these huge what you would call pruning shears, like your mom might use to cut down bushes, on the second to bottom step. He locked my other ankle to the other chain drilled into the wall, and then He walked back upstairs. He took the scissors with Him. He always took the scissors with Him.

He would come back down the steps carrying this huge full-length mirror mounted on two feet. The feet were wooden and shaped like cat's paws. Paws that faced forward and paws that faced back. He pulled the scissors from His back pocket and put them on the same step as before. Then He put the mirror a step or two in front of me. He did this so perfectly and without any extra steps or moves that thinking back I bring to mind a really great professional basketball player. Like that one who everyone is saying is the best shooter ever.

Yes, I know what some of you are thinking. I will not try and convince you otherwise. Of course I did try. And by this I mean in my mind. I mean, He was right there. And the mirror was way out of reach no matter how hard I tried or in which direction I tried to lunge. He made sure of this, and He paid attention when I was growing, making sure to move the mirror bit by bit so that it was the same distance away. I am not saying He was Willy Wonka. But yes. His mind was like a ruler.

And then it was like He went and got embarrassed. He got and He handed me the scissors and then He returned to His stairs. He walked backward. He knew that I knew I was in plain sight. He knew that I knew that He was in plain sight. He did not sit down. But He did His best not to look at me, and by that I mean the parts of me that were not holding the scissors. When I did catch Him looking at anything other than the scissors, He would be looking at my chest, and He would be looking at my belly, and He was looking as if seeing a young girl's belly was this brand new thing. His face was like a blue sky when there were no clouds.

After my first lesson, I learned to take off what you would consider about an inch. But I worked slowly. First, this was because I was nervous. His idea of teaching being of course not fun. But then, when I knew what I was supposed to do, cutting my hair was of course once in a while, this really rare thing, Him only having me cut my hair when He felt I needed to. And so, because this was just something different to do, I would work really slow, this of course being something interesting and not too much different than it would be for any girl in some ways, believe me or not, and me pretending like I was practicing what He taught me, and as I got older this was also time for me to figure out, when it came to escaping, or getting out, if there was something different I could possibly do.

Some of you think that you would think about getting out all of the time. And maybe you are right. At least in a little way. But that was only for a little while. For me, this is to say. Because let us just say you spend just twenty-four hours, as opposed to twenty-four hours times whatever number, straight, by which I mean without any breaks, chained up and sitting on your mattress. Or not chained up, looking out your window. What happens is that thinking, after a while, becomes this difficult thing to do. As in not in the way you are thinking. This is not to say you do not think, because of course that's impossible. And you'll just have to believe me when I say that I have tried. But what happens to you is you sort of become alive in this different way. By which I mean that thoughts and ideas, which by that I mean more than anything these sorts of pictures, well they sort of just pass on through you. And you can stop and you can look at whatever you want to. The problem with that though is that once you do, you are thinking in the normal way, which, as I just said, is no longer this easy thing to do.

It is not an idea of, Will it go round in circles?

No.

The question is, When will it stop?

My mom was, and still is, an anchorperson. And this for this very big channel for this very big city. Of course when He stole me she took a lot of time off work, and she spent all of her time with my dad and a group of people wearing gray, which is my favorite color, trying to find me. Hanging up signs and gray ribbons. But even stupid people know that at some point, as sad as it is, you have to give up. That of course things other than hope, which never ran out, at least for my mom, eventually run out. The main one of those things being time. By which of course I mean money. And my mom and my dad and these people were not dumb.

My mom was on the news every weeknight. And before He stole me I pretty much watched her on TV every single day. Because of this, even though I did not try, it was simple remembering what she looked like, and what she sounded like. But I did not remember what she smelled like, or what she felt like. And so I found myself, at least at first, thinking of her just sort of randomly. And then I sort of stopped doing that, and I just remembered having a mom. And after a while it was not as though I stopped missing her, it was just that like with all of my feelings she just became one of them. Of course some of you don't believe me, but it really is true.

Over time I still had feelings, I am not saying anything different. It was just that each and every feeling was connected with what you consider memory, and that, in time, this, which is to say my memory, became sort of like a snowball. By this I mean it was not getting bigger like you see on TV cartoons, when a tiny snowball at the top of a mountain gets set to rolling down, which is to say the side of the mountain, and gets bigger. No. This snowball was already made, and time was the sun. It, by which I mean the sun, never got too warm, or should I say the snowball never stayed fully cold, so it, the snowball, sort of melted down and down to freeze over again and again every moonlit night to become this one hard thing. When I did wonder about things, because it was impossible not to, I always ended up feeling the van's windows, or I smelled His scissors, and before long everything was that much harder and everything pretty much meant nothing to me, which is to say to that my memories, which are different than thoughts, mattered about as much as a rock matters to the wind.

After I killed Him, and escaped, I was pretty much ghost white, even though my dad is part Black. Now, by which I mean when you are reading this, my skin is sort of golden. For a while this was the most controversial thing about *Dry The Rain*. Not the fact that they showed, at least mostly, what He did to me with the potato peeler. Or for that matter the meat thermometer, so far as the gross out stuff goes. The people making the series, which is to say the producers and the writers, well they did something with the cameras, or whatever, so that Imogen Appleton's skin looks more like mine. She is just as white as a piece of computer paper, and so a lot of people were angry about this. Or at least they said they were. Which, if you know what I mean, and you should, you not having been locked up for whatever number of years, and having the time to listen and to think about these things, by which I mean these ideas. This is what I think.

If you care, and by that I mean if your mind is open and you are willing to listen just as much as you are willing to speak, it matters. No one should go around looking to have their mind changed. No. Of course not. I do not mean this at all. The people who do care know that this is something that however unlikely just might possibly happen, and those are the people I do not have a problem with.

Now before you go thinking anything, this does not mean that I immediately just go out and start having all sorts of or even small problems with all of the other people out there. I do like people. Most of them, I imagine. This story is just not about that. By which I mean I am not defensive. And I am not on purpose offensive. More yes than less I just do not possibly know or have any possible idea of what I should be thinking, and so I do not spend any of my time trying to guess. There are just so, so many people is the one thing I have really learned. And that is just talking about the people on the Internet, the people I see on the street. That, and it is really, really hard knowing any more than just a couple of them. By which I mean a few. And so that is where I spend my time and energy. And, if you listen to anything that I have to say, that, in my opinion, is what you should do, too.

.  .  .

Should a white girl play a Black girl on a TV show or in the movies?

At first I thought this question was weird even more than I thought it was stupid, and I definitely thought it was stupid. Stupid as in more than it did not make sense to me, I could not understand why it should even matter to make sense to me. That I will state was stupid of me, and that it is also interesting learning not just how people learn, but how people think. Because all I was thinking was that an actor was an actor, and that if a certain person who could act really well happened to look a lot like me it would be stupid not to use that person if she wanted to act me. By which I mean to take the part of Mallory. Which I also learned for actors, at least some of them, has to do with even more than something like money.

While it is dumb, and I will stay by that thought, I do understand why people do care. People told me the why, and in whatever way I am able I do understand that for a long time things were horrible, and if you do not know what I mean this is because you do not want to and so I am not going to waste any of my time on you.


If you were to ask me, which I do not know why some of you would because you will just say I am wrong, or will post that you do not believe me, the hardest part about coming back after Him stealing me is figuring out what I am permitted to have thoughts and feelings about, and what sorts of things people fight and argue about, and whatever I am not supposed to think about, and so what I do not do is try and figure them out. Those things I am allowed to have an opinion on and those things which, according to you, I cannot. And so I care about what I find interesting because what is most fair, by which I mean to say that which is just and true, well, this is never going to be found out or discovered while I am around and, I hate to say it, while you are around, too.


The dumb thing they did, and by them I do of course mean the producers and the writers, was going and coloring Imogen's skin and trying to make her look Blacker, which is something that I guess that I am, which is to say Blacker-looking, at least compared to her. Which the producers and the writers of course did not admit was true, by which I mean coloring Imogen, this being something that they denied and so people said they, the producers and the writers, did this just to get people talking while other people said they, the producers and the writers, did this to try and make this point, and that point being that what happened to me was not about anyone being Black or white, because He would have taken just anyone. Well, that is just a stupid idea and a talk for some other day, and because I have no idea what they were thinking I will tell you what I do not know and what I did not get and that is this.

People thought I was Black. And so this is where it gets confusing and strange and just overall weird for me. For a while this was not something anyone knew. My mom is as white as Imogen. She is as white as a loon. And my dad. Well, if you have not seen him, he only looks what might be considered Black if you know he is Black and are really thinking about it and looking to see his Blackness, which, again, is one thing I just do not get because why would you. That is like looking for an extra piece to a puzzle that has already been put together correctly. And one thing I have learned that I can say, because I am Black, is that he is as Black as, say, fill in the blank, and so I will say wet sand, while all that you can say is, if you are not Black, is that he is Black. I don't see how that rule solves anything.

So my guess is that the producers and the writers, those producers and the writers who, for whatever reason, but let us say money, cared about *Dry The Rain*, had no clue he was even Black, and that they made Imogen look dark just because I can get so tan and then someone, like always, with too much time on their hands, went out and found out that my dad was Black and posted online that *Dry The Rain* made Imogen look darker to represent the Black part of me which even I didn't know about until reading about part of the show and then asking my mom. Which, before you text or say anything, does not mean anything, and by that I mean at all, because in fact I wanted to ask my dad, he just was not home. Some things really are as simple as that.

At first, the producers and the writers, well, they were just really worried. Because remember, in case you forgot, *Dry The Rain* is based on real and actual events. And whoever found out and posted about this, by which I mean about my dad and him being Black, well they did this after the first or second episode aired, by which I mean the show was already on TV, and, more than this, *Dry The Rain* was, like, the biggest success. And this in so many ways, one of them being the producers and the writers swearing that the story was not made up, but based on real and actual events. And so the show was as big as anything on TV, as big as anything MovieTrap ever made. And so while this, by which I mean me being Black, has nothing to do with the show, what it showed was, like, this gap. People, by which I mean critics, could watch and point and say, See, it didn't happen exactly that way. They, which of course is to say the producers and the writers, did not even know that she, by which they mean me, was Black. And what is a bigger deal than a person not being Black? So of course they, by which I mean many of you, looked and pointed and said, What else did they make up? What else did they invent?

And sure it is still going on, by which I mean this and these other huge online fights, but what can I possibly say? This is a world where people answer questions that are not even asked. By which I mean raised. And how people word what they say as if they are stating questions. And how people go on talking, it is like they are standing in front of microphones. And by that I mean all of the time. As if there is no other way. And that if you sort of say that maybe there is, by which I mean another way, like perhaps one that is courteous, they get all crazy. You are going to think what you are going to think, and I do, despite how this might read, try not to judge you because one, I hate judgment and two, I just don't know how to. By which I mean judge. All that I can say is that I do care. About me. And, for real, about you.


The only time He ever got upset and by that I mean sad, as opposed to angry, was if my nose was bleeding or if a finger got crooked from being broken or when one of my eyes swelled shut. He was good at making fingers straight again. But you could not unswell an eye. And He was afraid, even scared I would definitely say, of blood. I could not understand that at first. Which is how I learned that He did not want to make me not so pretty, and gave me some of my first ideas about how I might possibly escape. Which was not something, as I have told you, that I thought about all of the time.


For all the things He was, He was not careless. And believe me when I say that that is way different from being careful.

You would think that after all that time I might have earned His trust. That He would not have felt the need to keep me chained to the wall, by which I mean at all. As in ever. There really was no need. At least for most of the time I was there. But for all the things He was, He was also not what you would call sadistic in some ways. I mean of course it is impossible knowing the whys of so many things, and, unlike you, I do not try to figure any of them out, but He did not get happy from having me chained. This is because it was not good for my body. But like I said, He was smart. Of course He would have been dumb to trust me. I mean of course. I know what many of you are thinking, but, whatever it is, you are wrong. He was ever careful. And so when I was not penned up outside drying the rain I was, way more yes than less half of the time, shackled and chained to His wall. That could take a toll.

This is true. Like you see on *Dry The Rain* there were cameras pointed at me. Five? That is what they say. So who am I to say. Only for me, which is to say in real life, this was just a little bit different. For me there was only one. But whatever. There might have been twenty. What does it matter? After I killed Him, I did not go upstairs and start looking around His house to discover what it was He did. As a matter of total fact, right after I killed Him, I was not in this huge hurry to do much of anything. All of a sudden, by which I mean once I was free, which is something different entirely, I could do whatever I wanted. This did not make sense to me. I know, I know. You would have gone to Taco Bell. You would have gone ice skating. I do not feel bad for you, but you just can't possibly see.

. . .

You know from watching *Dry The Rain* that there was a sensor or something on my chain that activated, or went off, whenever I moved more than to just adjust myself in more than just the, or I guess I should say a, basic way. And He gave me a lot of freedom when it came to adjusting myself, by which I mean there was a lot I could do before the sensor started to blink. I cannot say, exactly, what it did, other than it started blinking. But even I know there was more.

And no. By now, I think it is Episode Four, what they have titled *Total Despair*, the one that has just aired, or the episode that they are teasing and saying you will soon be able to see, and you have probably said to one of your friends, or your husband, or half the time just to yourself, that you would have hanged yourself. That you would have because He did, you would say, give her scissors, escaped by killing yourself.

And you are not wrong.

Because in time I do escape.

But you, at least those some of you who have been made, by which I mean conditioned, to consider these shows, by which I mean my ordeal, as a, say, story, something to sit and watch for fun, or as a way to be interested or at the least not bored, are even now while reading this busy poking holes in my story. Which I do get, because what happened to me is not a story. For example, I am alive. So there is no end. Yet.

Anyways. Somehow, as if I did not try, even if by trying I mean by thinking how to, one-hundred thousand times, you would have climbed the fence. You would have, as if I was dumb and not able to do so, found a way inside the van and then beeped on the horn until help arrived. Really? With Him home you would have honked on His horn until what? Someone heard you, by which I mean me, and came to my, by which you mean your, rescue?

To that, all I can say is: Please.

You, some of you would say. You already told us that He

wanted to keep you. That He did not want to hurt me. That I was safe.

But I already told you. He was, except for that one time, perfectly careful.

And even that might have had nothing to do with me.

With either of us.

And yeah, right. Safety.


He gave me a dictionary. Or should I say, He let me keep the dictionary that was down there. In His cellar. My home. There are many things I can tell you that you would find surprising. Facts and truths that are not in *Dry The Rain*. For example, I am not remarkable. He is not remarkable. You, on the other hand, are almost certainly remarkable. This is because remarkable, like memorable, are neutral words, and can be combined with negative events as well. So, He is anything but remarkable. I am anything but remarkable. While you and people like you will forever remain remarkable.

I do not expect you to understand.

This is because you would have to want to.

And I do not blame you, because it is impossible to know what you want to understand when you are sure that what you think you want is right.


Boredom is not as possible as people say. There were more things, way more and many things I was when He had me, other than bored. And think about this. Just think about the number of books written about boredom. And here I am not even talking about books like you would read in school if you were studying psychology, but novels. Books about boredom that people wrote as stories for other people to read for fun.

Or to make them sound like smart and important writers. There are many stories about people interested in the idea of boredom. One book is apparently so good that its writer killed himself before he finished writing. And so other people took care of the ending for him. I'm not exactly sure if that's true, or, if it is, what it means, if so. But it definitely means something.

This, the dictionary stuff they talk about, by which I mean show, in *Dry The Rain*, is not in any way right. It is impossible though because they are trying to make something boring, by which I mean watching a young girl as young as me read a dictionary, interesting. Plus, and this was for super real, they, the producers and the writers, relied on what I was telling them, and this was not much of anything because you go ahead and try and describe something as interesting as someone reading anything, not to mention something that is not even a story, and see how well you do. So what happens is *Dry The Rain* makes me look smarter than I am, instead of showing how tough I am, and what I did with the dictionary was pretty much just read and added, by which I mean in addition to how I was living, a different way of learning how to think.

Like, I have the perfect words for all sorts of things. Once you learn how to speak and write English, learning English is like learning another language once you really get into it. Now that I have killed Him, which you all will see in Episode Nine, which they give the most great title *Kill Him Till He Dies*, and once I left the place, this naturally being Episode Ten, called *Dead Alive*, well, all this time later I am trying to be an Anglicist, with the big major goal of working at a university library. Not a famous one but, like, a strange one. Like Widener. Or Whitman.

. . .

This is interesting. *Dry The Rain* is different from a lot of those popular MovieTrap shows because instead of the producers and the writers making and filming as they went along some sort of schedule, the show was all sort of produced and written and done all at once. By which I mean over this period of time they filmed every single episode before MovieTrap showed anything. This makes *Dry The Rain* basically like this new kind of series. This is part of what they, by which I mean MovieTrap and the producers, called innovation. They, which is to say MovieTrap and the producers, promoted, and still do promote, by which I mean brag, or say, how nothing like this has ever been done before, or, to be safe, at least in this way, which is something that so many people would believe, even me, even knowing they could be lying. This is because it is easy to think people cannot lie about big things, and it is not easy but it is important to many people, even now, to believe that people are not lying. Even though you, by which I mean we, know differently.

Another part of this, in terms of filming all at once, was because they wanted me watching. As in before airing a single opinion. By which I mean episode. They wanted to hear what I said. But me watching was not part of my contract. Like, for them, it was this huge mistake. They just assumed I would want to watch. They thought I would say Yes, and watch all of the episodes before they aired episode One.

But no.

All I did sign was this agreement promising that I would answer questions based on what had happened to me. Oh yes, of course and for sure they tried to sue us, by which I mean me, but words are not just words, they become something altogether different when they are written out and printed. And my parents did not sue back, but they threatened to. What is more, they said they would go public with MovieTrap's desire to subject me, a minor survivor, to more PTSD. So they, by which I mean the producers and the writers, did not know what I saw. Or, to be most precise, I should say they did not know what I didn't see. By which I mean viewed.

Like I have said, after I stopped watching, I am not sure what they say about me doing to Him or saying to Him. Although I do turn it on every once in a while. But that is just because I am curious to learn if they have made any changes about me being Black, by which I mean Imogen more than Mallory, which is what I have heard, by which I mean read, they are doing. But, to be honest, I think that's impossible. And I don't even know that much about this day and age.

You could tell me why you like these sorts of shows. Those hour-long *Dateline Specials*. Those commercial free programs you pick from your Rokus because who has the time for those, which is to say commercials, breaking up your narrative dream. Those episodes of *On The Case With Paula Whatever* that are on cable TV.

Mine, which is to say if *Dry The Rain* was a show, which by that I mean one episode, is not as bad as so many others, maybe even all of the others that I am aware of. This is because I am still here, by which I mean I live. I am alive. I survived. And other than those shows with Survive in the title, I am not sure they make TV shows where the person survives. Maybe this is because no one does. Survive, I mean to say. That I do not know. But these sorts of shows that I do despise are not books. And so people are not watching and waiting to feel happy. I have no clue what, exactly, they are turning on their TVs and watching me to feel. It's sad for me to say what I think the answer is. By which I mean to say entertained.

But the shows that take the rapes, sodomies, and murders of little girls and boys, or that take the housewife with the dentist husband who shoots her in the face expecting it to look like a suicide, or the woman on the houseboat who puts antifreeze in her boyfriend's leftovers while waiting to be added to his will, or the soldier who strangles the married woman with pantyhose because she said she was pregnant and was going to tell his, whatever, soldier boss that he raped her. Those sorts of shows that take people's real-life tragedies and turn them into hobbies that married people watch at bedtime. These Whodunit's, even though the killer has been caught, the crime totally solved. Those shows that pull and drag all sorts of innocent people through the mud and shovel salt into open wounds. How producers and the writers get people even though they are in jail, and by this I mean for life, and put them in a nice button down shirt and sit them in front of us with this green screen background that is imaged up so that it could be part of an office so that you get to guess, while you follow the show, if they were found guilty or innocent, because being guilty or innocent has nothing to do with it, what matters to you is the jury. What they found. By which I mean determined.

And these shows, how they talk about the mystery, and how that person is innocent, even though he is not, so that the show is like a story, something like a movie with a beginning, a middle, and an end.

Why?

What is the good in a show like that?

There is not any goodness, friends. No one even tries to pretend. That might be the point. Even in the world there is not a lot of good to come by. So it must be nice to consider these shows like little kids, by which I mean boys and girls littler than me, and think of them as bedtime stories. Falling asleep, and not even feeling badly for others but good for yourself because you are comfortable and have comfortably passed away some time and maybe, if you were lucky, entertained.

And not that I necessarily even want to, because I mean look at me, I cannot, for me having the lack of a better word, judge those people who, left surviving, go about in whatever way they want telling their stories. But what about the people who, by dying, or who in some other way do not get a say. Although, and many of you say otherwise, and that is fine, that is okay, but I would never put my face in front of a camera. I would never, other than what I agreed to do for my parents, put my voice near a recorder. And I can tell you this. I would bet none of those totally what you should call forlorn and lost mothers or fathers or best friend cousins or sisters or brothers were given money that adds up to over many million dollars. With options. They are in some other way, which is a story for another day, convinced. And that is sad, I say.

His cellar is fascinating. Of that, I think we all agree. The reason why His cellar interests me is because I do not understand it. I will try and explain this. By this I mean both the cellar and the reason why, after all that time, I do not understand it. His cellar. My home.

Even when I was there, by which I mean as opposed to

what you are thinking, by which I mean you think I am talking about my memory as in me really trying hard to remember the cellar just so that I can tell you what it was like. Well. Even when I was there, being in the cellar was like being in this strange city. At the bottom of these steps. Which is to say those steps. His eight stone steps. At the top of which was His always-closed heavy wooden door.

It is a circle, the cellar. That is the main thing you should have picked up from watching *Dry The Rain*. Not just that it was stone. That the stone is carved into this very specific shape. This is what should have jumped out at you. Instead of bothering yourself with the idea that there was that one window and how I was an idiot for not managing to escape.


We do not really have cellars in Virginia, and even further down south they are there even less so and if you are from there, or have been reading about what is not true online, I know what some of you are thinking. You are thinking that I am an idiot, by which you mean that it doesn't matter how old I am because I have the mind of a kid, and that this, where I was, because the one thing at least you do agree with, that you do believe, was that I was stolen and that He had me, was not a cellar, but, instead, like you have seen on TV, that it was a homemade dungeon, or a lair, or some other thing He built for His girls like me.

That, or that I was not in Virginia. For some reason a lot of people, despite this being exactly wrong, think He kept me in Pennsylvania.

I do not care.

I have seen enough cellars on TV and I have a lot of family up north. And so, when visiting family, up north, even on places like Long Island, which of course is surrounded by water and so is just like living down south and especially near the shore, it does not help to have a cellar. This is because of flooding. No one likes to dry the rain. Still. I have been to enough places and have seen enough places to know my home, which is to say where He kept me, was a cellar. This is because I have been in many different cellars. Which is something that I only do if the situation is extraordinary and or completely necessary. And while I'm sure He lived in that house for a long time, like maybe since He was a kid, I know the cellar was beneath a really old house and that that place was there way before Him.

What I could not reason out was why the cellar was, by which I mean is, a circle.

This is not part of my story, but it is part of *Dry The Rain*, and this is one neat thing I learned before I stopped watching. Well, to be exact, I still, as I have said, tune in once in a while. Which is how I learn certain things. Many of you say I could go and type questions into the Internet, but the Internet is as reliable as a liar. But I have trouble with TV and following stories anyways, so some of this might be wrong.

I don't meet with as many people as before, but of course I still see this psychiatrist, and she, Dr. Anastasio, whom I will, I suppose, talk more about later, said that a group of explorers, well I guess they were more than explorers, they were anthropologists, what she said were called the cultural kind and they were exploring the Amazon jungle, deep where of course people lived but where no white person ever visited. Or so they said.

So these men, then. By which of course I mean these white men. What happened was they came across a group of undiscovered peoples and one of the things that they did was show them a TV. It was connected to a DVD player. Do not ask me what was on the DVD because Dr. Anastasio said nothing when I asked her, she just sat there staring and what you would call faintly smiling, gold glittering from the small glittering gold crucifix she was always wearing, so I of course have no clue. The people, who had never even seen a lightbulb, could not see what was on the TV. The movie. Or whatever they were watching. Their brains could not figure out how people could be inside a box and so instead they just saw nothing. They told the explorers not even that they saw color but a bunch of black and white shapes. They described what they saw as black and white rainbows.

That, for them, is basically how things are for me.

In their shapes most cellars are like rectangles. Or squares. This of course makes sense. This I did understand, or felt I knew to be true. How, or should I say why, these places are squared. Because picture what rises from them. Houses. And how many times have you walked past a house whose shape was not more yes than less a rectangle. A square. I know, I know. You can. But it is uncommon. It's rare.

A long time ago a lot of people believed not in people like Him, which was too far out and unbelievable, but they did believe, and totally, in witches. Or, to be even more exact, if there was a person like Him, he would be thought of as a witch. As opposed to a Him. These people thought that witches would live in their cellars. I know. Weird.

Anyways, what these people did, it being this known fact that witches hid in corners, what they did was make their cellars not squares, but circles. This way the witches had nowhere to hide. This is so amazing and funny. Of course I am different and look at things differently as well, but one thing I think more than others is that people, as in most, are nice. Good, even. But based on what I know, and given that now how I am forced to learn things, so many people are actually not very smart, by which I mean it is fair to say so many people are, if not dumb, ignorant. Or, perhaps to be more precise, gullible.

Other than me and a few other things, the cellar was nothing but stone, and the stones were nothing but cool, gray, and smooth. It was not a dungeon, but you would insist it was because of all you have seen on movies, TV, and, especially, cartoons. And yes. The way that the rocks, which were like these small round boulders, were cemented all together, all flattened out, this did make the cellar look like a dungeon. But trust me, it was not.

Here is one memory I had in the beginning. And because of that, by which I mean because this memory was part of the beginning, this is something I remembered, and always will remember, and has become something I think of clearly. This memory will become more important later. Trust me. And, for what it is worth, this is another something only you get to see, by which I mean know, because you are taking the time to read this.

I was at Our Lady of Sorrows, the church where my parents took me, standing inside the sacristy. It was not much of a room. But I liked it. The room felt full of different. Of possibility. It, too, by which I mean the sacristy, had one pretty big window. At least I thought so. It was big enough for me to crawl through. And because the sacristy was beneath the ground, this meant I would not have fallen out the window but crawled up, through, and out onto the ground. Just like His cellar. But more than anything there was, inside of the sacristy, just like His cellar, all of this open space and this made you believe that there was room for something amazing to happen.

.   .   .

And yeah so the walls, the ceiling, and the floor were stone. Only the window was not at all stone. Because just about all of this was underground it didn't matter, but you could tell the walls and the ceiling were thick, which of course made it basically impossible for sound to escape or enter. But this must have mattered at least some, because you could see these areas where He took time to caulk cracks. The entrance door from inside the house and the exit door to the back yard where I would go to dry the rain were, like, whatever, wrapped, or to be more precise I guess I should say filled, with all of this rubber to prevent sound from passing through or around the doors. Like me, He did not want anything leaking.

There is no such thing as silence. This is because once you hear silence, by which I mean what you think is silence, you soon hear sounds. You learn that silence is impossibility. That there is no such thing as nothing. Birds can help with what to listen for. After spending hundreds of hours watching birds with this incredibly thick glass blocking out their chirps and songs, and you do not hear so much of what you are seeing, you start to get better at understanding. And not just about birds and why they do the things that they must do, but all sorts of concerns.

When you are free and not chained to a wall, and if you are interested in birds or maybe even birding, the thing to really figuring out and learning all about a bird's sound is to get as close to the animal as possible. I would say that doing this is even better than listening to a recording. Being able to identify different birds, which is the goal of most birders, is pretty useless. And by this I mean you know what birds are which birds simply by knowing their songs. It is like knowing a girl is in trouble simply because you hear her scream. What you have to learn how to do is make something of information. This is because human beings are capable of telepathy. Constant, the transfer of information. What it comes down to is a matter of tuning in.

Of course you say. Yeah, right.

Which I get.

But it is true how your mind, if, like your eyes, you let it unfocus, by which I mean you just sort of space out, it will act just like invisible antennae, picking up unseen vibrations. And if you do not believe me, you do not have to take my word for it. You can, if you want, consider birds. How they flock and fly together. How they amass as if only to fly together, rising and falling upon the wind to lift as one and ride upon some naked wave of wind high, and then higher, into the blue, un-shattered sky.

But what I will also say is this. So like birds, so like bees. What I am saying by that is this: Early on, this is to say in the beginning, when I found out I was interested in things, and that I was not just a memory, I began considering birds, by which I mean every kind of bird out there in front of me, to be most exact and particular, as bird. Let me explain.

I have not been in love, and I do not know if I will ever fall in love. But I imagine what happened to me down there in His cellar was something like that. By which I mean I was out of control. My feelings had me. Which is what love must be.

For a while birds were something interesting only because they were better, and by this I mean much better, than looking at nothing. And then one day, when I was watching birds, by which I mean any one bird, there is no way I could tell you which, I became different, and the reason for this was because I was smiling.

When you smile your brain sets off all these tiny molecules, which I guess are chemicals and what scientists call neuropeptides. And so now of course, well more in the beginning, after I killed Him and then escaped, but still, back in the beginning, everyone, but especially the doctors, by which I mean the psychiatrists, the people who were paid to not leave me alone, they wanted me smiling. If I was smiling, other chemicals, like dopamine and endorphins and serotonin, well, apparently, those would fill me up and get me to feeling good as well. Or, at the very least, not so bad. There was even medicine for this, they said. By which of course they meant pills.

One of them, by which I mean a doctor, or a psychiatrist, it totally and absolutely doesn't matter which, wanted to know why I didn't want to take pills, which they insisted on calling medicine.

The truth was I didn't know, by which I mean since I wasn't sure that doing something, like taking pills, was definitely going to be good for me, there was no sense in pill-taking at all. After whenever they talked about taking pills, pill-taking, they always told me, might produce some undesired effects, which of course they thought I was too dumb to understand meant side-effects, which, forever and always are, by definition, bad, if not terrible. But I did not want to give them the opportunity to not trust me, to have an open door to come through and correct me and, without saying so, insist that I was broken, and damaged, and that pills were not much different than tape, or glue, and for me not to trust them was precise and exact proof of this. So I said, by which of course I mean I typed, I don't know.

You don't know what, sweetie?

What my mom thinks, I typed.

Well, what does your dad think?

The same thing.

The same thing as who, sweetie? Me?

No, I typed. My mom.

I don't understand, the person, a she, said.

They don't know what's best for me, I typed. That's why they trust me to see you.

These people, by which I mean every doctor and shrink, I haven't met one of them who doesn't like to be flattered. Especially by me. Who, because, according to all of them, I am so incredibly damaged and broken, I am this puzzle who, in solving, they will earn all of this extra attention and accolades. And yes I am leading them on, but it is not mean or cruel because I don't want pills, I don't want to become medicine.

Really? they said, smiling, looking off at anything but me.

I nodded.

Well, she said.

For real, I typed.

But she did not hear the ping. She just sat there, dreaming.

But, and this I did not even try telling them, by which I mean any of the doctors and the psychiatrists, I did not feel bad. I didn't tell them not because I knew they would not believe me, which of course they would not, I didn't tell them because they, as always not really listening, would take me saying I did not feel that bad as there being something even more wrong with me. That I was even worse than they all feared. Because I would be crazy not to feel bad after everything He did to me. And so I knew they would color me crazy. By which of course I mean crazier. And so no, I did not tell them about birds. Or, to be more exact, this one bird, which soon became my bird. And I knew this was my bird because I was not smiling because I felt good. I was smiling because I understood.



Once I understood, by which I mean I knew how I could go about killing Him, I thought back to before, which of course is something I always tried to ignore. I could really only remember pigeons, seagulls, crows, and robins. And this only kind of. By which I mean in this basic, general way. I doubted everything. Anyways, I mention these birds because more than most they were the birds that were around even if it was not raining. More than anything, I could not remember feeling. By which I mean to say any one way. About any one thing. Sort of like how I remembered, by which I mean thought of, birds.

But the thing about birds. From the very beginning, birds dropped from the sky. They fell heavy as pennies to, only at the last moment, sort of lift, which is to say rise up. And then, and this is all in the same motion, they slowed in this way I don't have the words for, before, just for a moment, they stopped. They landed on His fence. They dropped from His fence and they hopped and they bounced around His backyard. They did this a lot after it rained, by which I mean the hopping and the bouncing around His backyard. Of course they flew away as soon as my door opened. At first.

But there were other birds. There were many other birds, pretty animals I saw for the first time. Animals that I instantly loved. Even the cardinals were larger and bigger and brighter. What you would call vibrant. And then came what I have since identified as the Eastern Bluebird. This little fellow. With his small, round head and his big, round belly? And this not to mention his gentle demeanor and pleasing manner of being? He was so cute. I was drawn to him. And that blue. This color was so amazing it was like they, by which I mean the birds, became so blue so as to blend with His backyard's high liquid-blue sky. It is only when you experience so few emotions that it becomes possible to excite within yourself such incredible passion, and of course many of you would say this is impossible, that nothing good could ever come from being with Him. But of course you would have to care and you would have to pay attention to understand what I am saying, not to mention what I have not said, and never would. Which I know is hard to do.

I studied my bird. Not so much interested in its colors, which, quite naturally, I began taking for granted, so much as its behavior. Those ways and the means by which he passed through each and every day, how he moved far more frequently than people, and with much more purpose, to do so much less. I thought all about what was so important in what little he did. Look how he turned his head. Isn't it crazy, the whip of a wing. I saw how simple it is to see, to understand by way of body how he used so much less. To become some other thing. Something greater. And so yes, it was around then when I understood not how, but that I could escape. Which of course is not something they, by which I mean the producers and the writers, cared to ask me about. Let alone show. By which I mean Mallory watching birds. On TV.

When chained, which of course wasn't all the time, and which even He knew was unnecessary, because, really, where was I going to go, I was chained beside the sink. My mattress was beside the sink as well, facing the steps leading to His kitchen. But for so long that was just a guess. Until I killed Him I did not know what was at the top of the steps. It could have been His living room. Or maybe it was just a really long hallway. It was sometimes interesting to guess.

Because only one foot was chained, usually, which of course was way better than having both feet chained, I had to learn how to arrange myself so that I was not totally uncomfortable and did not go about setting off His alarm. I had two pillows and two blankets. Just so you know the pillows did not have cases and they were made of this fabric, He had to have sewn them Himself, they were made of this material, like denim, that was impossible to rip open, which is to say in any way tear. Seriously. It was like they were made from this sort of soft lead. And the blankets were so thick they would never be ripped to work as a rope. A noose.

Because He stole me when I was so little I did not have much knowing to go on when thinking. The idea of killing myself was just a part of me as much as being creepy was a part of Him being Him. I did not think it was wrong. The idea was just there. So I do not know what this says about us people. What you might call humanity. I now think this was just because I did not want to be there. And I got to believing the only way that would be possible was if I was no longer alive, and of course the really fun part of thinking about this was that anywhere would be better than where I was and so I was in no way scared and more than what you would consider curious if not even willing, by which I mean excited. I guess the best word for this is hopeful. And even though I am of course religious I still do sort of think that is what Heaven is. Hope. But you have to have a lot of hope to be willing to die. And No, to answer your thought, of course God would not have punished me. I bet he would have been proud of me not for having something like faith, but for being brave.

You of course think I am making this up, but with so many questions I would ask you, Why?

If you think about it, I have already been paid. I have been and I am and I will and I always will be portrayed. I will forever be thought of a certain way. By you and by others. Nothing that I say matters. I talk about what interests me, sure. But more than that, like the idea of killing myself, I find myself talking about myself. All of those ideas and words are there before me. I slow down much of the time before speaking, by which of course I mean writing down my words, just to make sure that the words that come out of my mouth, by which I mean so to speak, are what I want to say, what I want people thinking and not necessarily exactly what I am thinking. Not because I think they, which is to say my words, are wrong. How could they be wrong? But I want to be sure that everything I say is something that I want heard. Because it is only with myself and my parents that I want to be okay. Well, them, Uncle Billy, and Mary.

He ran a dehumidifier. This was as far from me as possible and it was chained to the wall like a little girl. Anything around me that was not necessary was a risk and so of course I did not know why, but He figured the dehumidifier was necessary. I am pretty sure I know why. Maybe I will get into it. But what I can say is this. Other than me, if you know what I mean, He worked to make sure that nothing was ever damp. I know. Gross.

I liked the way it, this is to say the dehumidifier, hummed. It was like living inside a stone silo, His cellar, and I did not like it when the dehumidifier got filled up with humidity and went quiet. In the beginning I would howl. I think this meant I was sad. But at this point I take pride in the fact that I have not spoken in so long. You try spending so much time waiting and see what you end up being proud of. Words are pretty much unnecessary things. Spoken words are almost always not necessary. There being other ways. There being other means. By which I mean of communicating. Sounds like writers much better than me saying words are nothing more than stains on silence. Of course many of you are saying I am lying, or that I am demented, because I told all of those people about what happened so they could make *Dry The Rain*. But there are many ways of telling people something and only one of those is talking.

When you do not speak what happens is that after a while the words in your head do become much louder and clearer as well. Through all the years, by which I mean any point in time but, really, the time I was with Him, from the things I have never said, and probably will never say, there is nothing more important than what's going through your mind. Like they say, or at least this one guy I like, anyway, what he says is, If looks could kill, we'd both be broken. Which means a number of different things. To a number of different people. Depending on how you think about it.


There was the one window. This, you are right to think, was a stupid risk for Him. Only you are exactly wrong. This as well is one more reason why I know most of the girls He kept He did not keep at all and how I know that once He found me He sort of decided to retire. At least for however long He had it planned in His mind, Him of course not expecting me to kill Him. But I cannot care what you say or to whom you say what, He was incredibly careful. There was no way that window was for Him a risk. If it was, it, by which I mean the window, would not have existed.

. . .

The window was ground level. By the time I left the glass was five hands wide and two hands tall. In the beginning it was way more hands than that. I will say that yeah, this is a pretty big opening. Surprisingly big, even. So I do get what some of you are seeing. The window, though. It was sort of like in this melted way closed and the glass was inches thick. Looking back at it now I would say at least two. I know that you think you would find a way to break open the window and that this idea is something you believe even more after you see the lie that is *Fight or Flight* and that, somehow, even after you somehow freed yourself from the chain or chains and you had smashed open the window and with glass ripping open your chest and thighs and neck and feet you would squeeze out of the cellar and.

And that is the big and.

And what?

Leap over the fence? Run to the nearest neighbor? Flag down a car? Dig a hole under the fence? Tunnel your way out?

Listen. Don't you see? You don't. It's like so many of you simply lack windows. By which I mean this way of looking out of something, instead of through yourself, so that you can think. We don't need to place our minds on oven racks and set them to bake. We don't need, and I can tell you this, for sure, to lock ourselves away in a room and wrestle understanding from our nature. We just need nature. And to grow from that, naturally. And then you would remember that He left the basement door open. By which I mean unlocked. So the window. Were it a risk, to Him, it would not have existed.

Listen. Thank you. All of you who write me nice notes. Who post all sorts of positive things. You are out there. Your words exist. But they are not what I, and I am sure you, consider interesting. Worth reading about. So I am just writing down the silly stuff. Not to be obnoxious. And not to get you to read. Those, by which I mean the words I just wrote, are just some of the funniest things I have read and seen. And if you are wondering, the answer is No. I do not think about things like ratios.

I did not, but I can for sure tell you that some, that probably all of the others tried for sure. The window's frame was beaten and battered. The window's frame was sort of dented and scratched. At least in a way. And there were the fingernails. There were these long and faded blood trails. This was because these girls were never meant to dry the rain. Because of this, they saw the window as a means to escape. Everything had to happen somewhere, at some point, for something to happen. To have happened. But what does my truth matter when you have got all of the answers?

When I stood on my mattress I could look through the glass and see the backyard. Let me ask you this. Do you think of tomorrow like you think of today?

If you say yes, that is pretty much what looking out my window is like. I could jump or I could lie on my back and this gave me a different point of view. A way of looking at things. But the only true way of looking was standing on my feet and looking at what I could see. What was pretty inter-esting, thankfully, was that me looking through the window gave me the chance to look at the only thing growing on His little square of grass. A tree, I am pretty sure it is a pine, I killed Him and left before it got big enough for me to be sure just what it was, that began to grow, I have to be sure, acci-dentally.

.  .  .

The amazing thing is that when drying the rain I should have killed my tree. Any number of times once I understood, or learned, what I was doing, I should have uprooted and ripped my tree out of the ground which, of course, back then, was this tiny little thing I obviously did not even see but when I did it looked completely out of place, by which I mean like a tombstone in the middle of a playground. But no. I noticed nothing. I was still throwing pinecones into boughs and that, if you ask me, is why I think my tree survived. Nothing good ever happens. If something is considered good, something has to happen and we have to like it and think of it as being good. That is all. So, if it does, good happening I am trying to say, this has to happen by accident. In terms of us thinking and making it just so.

For weeks and months and maybe even a year I did not know anything was there and growing until a tiny tree, not even what you would consider an inch tall and maybe ten or maybe twelve steps from where I stood on my mattress to look out on something other than the cellar rose from my often enemy, the Earth. It was as soft as bits of trimmed hair around my feet. He gave me a dustpan and broom and from His seat on the steps watched me sweep up before taking the dustpan, brush, and broom back upstairs after having me cut my hair.

From then on and no matter what you think, for even more than me I hoped and prayed He did not kill my tree. By this point I was thinking about killing Him very much and so I was thinking about my mom and my dad a little bit more as well. Not a lot, but a little. And not so much about them, but how I would act if I ever saw them again. And so Him killing that tree would have killed me worse than He could have. I would have hated to have done something stupid when, so long as I was patient, I at this point really knew I would pretty soon get an opportunity to stick His scissors or something in His face and then His throat and then pummel Him while He bled, Him being terrified and scared of His own blood, unsure of what was happening, with me watching me kill Him until He died.

Of course He knew about my tree.


My mom and my dad do not tell me about anything of my life before Him and they do not tell me anything about Him unless I ask them, which means they do not tell me anything about Him. At first they tried, thinking it was a good thing like my counselors to pretty much just talk about anything, but of course when they saw how I was acting to their words they stopped. This got them to thinking that pictures were not a good thing. By which I mean looking at them and talking, or what they or you might say reminiscing about them. Here is something I will share with you that I do not think I have heard about even one person mentioning.

When in *Dry The Rain* they show the inside of my house. By which I mean basically the set. This is because the producers had these amazing professional workers build this super cool model of what the exact inside of my house looks like. The next time you are watching *Dry The Rain*, look at all of the pictures of anything. Either on a shelf or stand or on the wall or on end tables or dressers. You will see they are all paintings. There are no photographs. I could not say how many of them are original, but of course not too many. They are mostly just really nice prints. And all that is real. Before the producers could have a copy of my house made my parents took down pictures of anything to do with my family and so everything in my *Dry The Rain* house is a painting. I would bet money there is not a place like that anywhere else. Even in poor parts of the world I am sure there are at least drawings of the people who live in every house because this is human nature. And part of helping me get back to being anything near normal has a lot to do with getting rid of a lot of what we all, even most of you, would agree is human nature.

I was baptized as soon as I was able. By which of course I mean my parents had me baptised, by a priest, like when I was one or maybe two weeks old. Or maybe one or two months old. Either way. This is because, and this is where people who hate religion are right, at least in my opinion, the Church says that, thanks to Original Sin, you, when you are in your mother, belong to Satan. And you remain in what you, well, to be more precise, I should say them, by which I mean Catholics, that you will remain in state until baptism. That if you die before being baptised you are doomed. By which I mean your soul. And by which I mean forever. Eternally. But were that the Church's biggest mistake? I would take it.

Anyways.

After that, by which I mean after me getting baptized, it was going to church every Sunday and how the start of each new week was sort of based on that, by which I mean how Sunday was sort of set up just like a school day, with a set schedule and routines and well I really grew to like this, by which I mean church and Sundays and I know this must be true because what else would cause me to remember something like that. Which is what makes how I feel about Mary, including everything that happened, something I know to be true.

One thing I will watch on TV, although of course I do not go looking for it, just like I do not go looking for anything else on TV, is anything to do with near-death experiences. Now I know what many, if not most of you are thinking, and of course you are exactly wrong. I understand. Who am I to say? Because while the sun is warm, water is not wet. It is easy for us to confuse things. But I do know that at some point He was going to kill me. Either by accident or something He planned when I got to be more like a woman I did know that one way or another I was going to die. Or, to be more precise, I knew that one of us was going to die. This meant I had a set number of days. So this is not in any way a near-death experience. I mean given the situation, I was really healthy. This is weird and I do not have any way to know if this is even true but I am pretty sure that it is a fact that I never even got sick. By which I mean not even once. By which I mean a cold. A flu. As opposed to of course puking.

Even a near-death experience is the wrong way of putting all of this into words. For this to be real, by which I mean what I am talking about, the person involved is not near it, by which I mean death, the person involved is dead. Has died. The living people around this person totally and completely agree on this. And by people I mean doctors. And then that dead person somehow comes back to life. And it does not matter if it is for one second or for fifty-eight minutes. If a person is dead a person is dead.

One thing I have never looked up and never will is Marian apparitions. This is because that would be ruining something, personally. You of course might say that I am lying, that what is on *Dry The Rain*, whatever particular episode it is because of course I do not know, I cannot be sure because I have not seen that episode and the producers and the writers mess up the order of everything, is based on something I have read about or seen and told the producers and the writers who then made it this major important part of *Dry The Rain*. Like in a book Mary is a solution to a particular *Dry The Rain* plot or problem. But it is just like everything. You will never believe what you do not want to know.

Think, though.

As unpopular as God is, why would the producers and the writers even think to dream that up? But one thing I do know just by being alive is that many if not all Marian apparitions are similar. At least in how the stories come out. Sort of like the people who died, by which I mean to say those who had near-death experiences who then go on to live again so as to be able to talk about and tell their stories of all that happened and that all of them saying it being mainly all about that warm white light and how they feel totally and forever at peace and how they are floating somewhere in the same room with or at least where they can see their dead body and how they do not want to come back and the only reason they do, which is to say come back, is because some dead person they know and who they have been talking to tells them that this is not their time yet and to go on ahead and do so. By which they mean not die just yet. To keep on living. To float back down and into, or inside of, their bodies.

The thing with them, though, which is to say the stories more than the people, though of course the people matter as well, is that these people who do not know each other tell the same sort of story. They are dead and they come back and they all talk more yes than less about the same version of things happening. And then other people, like scientists or doctors or whoever, anyone who goes on to study the story, not the people, I mean I cannot be quoted on this because what do I know, but I have never heard of them studying such a wide amount of people, by which I mean the way they had died. Drowning. Heart attack. The bends. Falling from a ladder. Bear attack. What was common, though, was that everyone's heart stopped beating. At least from that point of view. So no one cares how they, by which I mean these people who had near-death experiences, got from living to dying.

But from there there are all sorts of things to consider.

How basically every person says they are there, floating above and looking down on their body.

How they feel so very happy and so very much at peace.

How they feel warm.

How they feel loved.

How, of course, there is that great, white light. And how, and very seriously and sincerely, they do not want to come back.

I, like you, believe them. But by that I mean I believe they believe what they are saying. That whether they saw the bottom of heaven or not, they think they did. Which is to say they think this helped them. By this I mean that the great white light was, like a person, like God, active. That the great white light had helped them.

Now when this is happening, and this is the same when people see Mary, do not get me wrong, I am not saying otherwise, because those people also are alone and of course we have to take them at their word. But when people die and then come back to life no one is studying their brains to see what happens. By this I mean in real time. Doctors are too busy trying to keep them from forever dying. So there is nothing to tell us why people feel and see the same thing.

And by that I mean basically. But definitely close enough if you ask me. I mean of course the shows I have seen do talk about studies. I know about a couple of the theories. I know about a couple of daytime TV shows. But there really are not that many. And by that I mean shows. Or theories. At least according to me.


It is different when you are talking about people who see Mary. Yes, people who see Mary know who Mary is, at least I think so, I think this must be true, because how else would they know who, by which I mean to say Mary, she is? But that could be a maybe not, because, like I have said, I have never read about them. Marian apparitions that is to say. And so these people, it is possible to think of things after real time, which is to say when it is happening, and scientists and doctors are able to study these people and not just put together what they report. Like in terms of what they knew about religion before all of what they saw and had seen. Or hook their brains up to machines. I guess what they know or what they had believed before seeing Mary is sort of important as well. To be honest, maybe that is the most important thing.

But what is more important if you ask me is that when people see Mary, Mary happens to them. Nothing crazy like dying happens in order for these people to be able to see. They might be walking in a field is what I am saying. Or maybe looking at water falling from a faucet filling a bathtub. They do not even have to be praying, which, while many people certainly think of as a crazy thing to do, is nothing like getting shot with a bullet. And then the next important thing is that unlike those among us who die and then say they have been born again and become in my opinion zombies, people who see Mary all see something different. And there is a kind of amazing and wonderful sort of magic in that.

Other than the producers and the writers, no one has ever asked me about Mary. My mother wants to. And she has, in her way, tried. But, to point out a fact, until about this point in time, I have never stopped to think about why. Which by that I mean the connection I feel towards and that I have with her. By which I mean Mary. A relationship that I know I have with her and have had with her ever since I was a little girl, long before He had anything to do with me. Because of course now I do think about her all the time.

What might be the most wonderful thing is that I think of her in color and of course this color would be blue. You will not, but I do hope that you try to think of her as, or of, Blue. I hope you will try not to think about this as some religion thing, and what you think about God or do not think about God, and just think about how I think about Mary as you would think about someone you love. Because that would be best. But if you cannot do that then just think about Mary like you would a really good friend. Even if you can just do that, that would be enough.

Even if you do not like Christmas you cannot get rid of the fact that so many people do and as part of that many of them go and they hang up their Christmas lights. And so every year you see these. By which I mean Christmas lights. Every year you have seen these and every year you will see these, love Christmas or leave Christmas. Think of those blue ones. By ones I mean lights. Most people do not go out and buy these and so if you see them you are most likely looking at the house of someone who has had these lights for a long time and for whom this color has a lot of extra meaning. Like maybe they got them from their grandmother, even. The big old-fashioned kind where if even just one light goes out all of the lights go out, the whole huge and long string of them. So you have to know which ones I am talking about because they stick out. The sort of most beautiful blue radiant antiques. Well you do not have to have to, but you at least know what I mean. And not that blue that is part of a string of colored lights. No. Not that. Or to be more exact, not those. This blue is that blue of just those strings of light that are just blue and very pale and so very pale they can in a way feel almost white. If you can picture that color in your mind you will now know how I feel about Mary. At least sort of.

Smiling makes you feel good. Why this is I could not tell you because I have no clue. When I do guess the best idea I have is that when we are happy, or, better yet, feeling good, we smile. So when we smile on purpose, no matter how we are feeling, our body is used to feeling good when we happen to be smiling from feeling good or happy and so we just feel that way, like how you yawn when you even think about the word yawn. Like how whether you admit it or not you, just now, this very moment, yawned.

This is how it is with me and Mary.

By which I mean it has nothing to do with science. With, whatever, peptides.

By how do you explain something like this to producers?

That this is how it is with me and Mary. How is this something you can possibly say, by which I mean explain, to writers?

Because yeah, for sure, they were interested, even if only because they were interested in everything I had to say, them, the producers and the writers, never knowing what might, or, more importantly, what might not be an important story from me to keep. And Mary and how I thought of her wasn't, at least it sure doesn't seem, like a story they thought was all that important, was some part of my ordeal that they really wanted the parts of from me to keep, because they only really asked me about her once, and even then it was very specifically, by which I mean they wanted to know what happened in my home, His cellar, as opposed to generally, which, really, is the only possible way to speak about someone like God. Like Mary. But of course they asked me about Mary, I'm not saying they didn't, and the conversation, more yes than less, went kind of like this, and it doesn't matter if I was talking to a man or a woman, a producer or a writer, because at many points, and this was one of them, they were all so not different from one another that they might as well have been the same person, saying the same things, only differently, which is something that I learned to do well.

She's never looked up Marian apparitions, someone said.

This was spoken after the people in the room, after however long talking, had what you would call lapsed into silence. That this silence in the morning is something I remember so well is of course because one, we were talking about Mary, but also because there was this word lapse which, just like any word, entered my mind, and I was sitting there not in any way bored, knowing that if I spoke, by which I meant literally spoke, I could bring them to their knees and while I knew that I never would, by which I mean speak, the idea was still amusing. Holding back my smile I got to wondering if it was correct that silence was something you, by which I mean anyone, could lapse into, because my thought, by which I mean understanding of the word, was that to do so was to make a mistake. That falling into that sort of silence was a temporary sort of failure. Yes, it was a mistake, by their ways of thinking, not to be talking. But them not talking finally seemed like the smartest decision they could make given that they might actually be thinking. I have no way of knowing, but if they were that meant they had finally done something correct. This is what I was thinking, by which I mean I was having thoughts along these lines, when this wonderful and terrific silence was broken, and I now know that no one was thinking. And that yeah, them not speaking was, to their ways of thinking, this total decline in standards. A slip that needed correcting.

No, someone said. She never said that.

Sure she did.

She never said that. No.

Well she's right here, guys, ask her.

I shook my head, No.

Well guys. We still have a bit of a Mary Problem.

Yeah, one way or another the kid gets out of the chains.

You sure, they say to me. You're positive you didn't just find a key on him?

All that talk about unlocking you. Maybe the Mary stuff was just, like, a dream?

I already told you, I type.

What do you mean?

What does she mean?

I type, He was perfectly careful. He of course never thought I had a chance, but still, whenever He came down to be with me He never brought keys. Never.

I'm not sure that makes sense.

Like, he, of course, must have. When letting her go.

How did he let you go, they said, without keys?

Ignoring them, I typed, Before I got free, when He came down to get me, it wasn't to unlock me. He didn't have keys.

This got them, the producers and the writers, all talking. About, eventually, what they agreed to be, by which I mean call, the Mary problem.

*Dry The Rain* isn't about that kind of salvation, they said.

No one wants to hear about God, they repeated.

Deep down though, like at the most important parts and levels, I knew they believed me. This is not to say they believed in God, or Mary, but that I believed in Mary, and God, by which I both do and don't mean that to them I was like how one of those near-death people are to me, and how this was something they knew to be true, and that, because of this, maybe this problem was necessary.

So, they said. It's obvious that you feel this profound connection. With Mary.

I nodded.

We can write that. There's no problem there.

I shrugged.

But for this to be different? To get people to really care? Well, they'll need to see what isn't there. Which—

What they're trying to say, someone interrupted. Listen. Kiddo. I know this must be tough. But this is really important. They looked around the room for support. This is going to be a must.

Really.

As in there is no other option, honey.

We just need you to do your best.

Your absolute best though.

Which shouldn't be too tough, though, right? I mean, given how much this meant?

Means.

She knows what I mean.

Does she?

So. Sweetie. Mary. Can you tell us? Very specifically. What did she look like?

How did she appear?

Don't worry about what you forget, okay?

That's right. Just tell us what you remember.

I think of her in color, I typed, then deleted.

Think of Christmas lights. Think of those blue ones, I typed, then deleted.

Can you picture color in your mind? I typed. I hit send.

I could tell by the way they looked at their phones, by which I mean their phones to them looked broken, that even if they could, by which I mean picture a color, a color was something that they couldn't picture in the way I was meaning.

There was a lot of talking.

I just listened because, by then, I knew there wasn't much I could possibly do.

I smiled. Because when it came to what I could possibly do, and how much, what else was there?

Of course who could ask for more. So do not make this come out wrong. Other than that one time with Mary it is not as though I can say she did something for me. As in like for me to point at specifically. What you would call proof. But the remarkable thing is that I know she has done so much for me it is of course not infinity, but you would need to count them, by which I mean the number of things she has done for me, on a city of fingers.


The thing to know is that I did not and have not and will not ever try. By which I mean I have never tried to call or to see Mary. Most of the time we all know we are loved and that we all have people who we love. I know that Mary loves me and she is a person that I love. Even right now or whenever I am thinking about her it is like the dead person floating over and looking down at their body. There is just this great feeling of peace. The best way I can describe it is like to imagine you are awake even though you are so safe and warm in bed asleep. It is not that. It is the feeling. Of not wanting to go back to any other feeling.


Once when I was home after I had killed Him and I was not talking to a psychiatrist but to this woman who reminded me of her. By this I mean the psychiatrist I had in mind. She was from our church, Our Lady of Sorrows. Not to be mean, but when you are talking about this day and time, not too much has changed. There are people like my mom and my dad, and especially my dad, because he is way more into going to church than my mom, and then there are others. Of course there are all sorts of people in-between, but you know what I mean. The others are the sort of people who always use the word Jesus in a sentence and sort of again not to be mean but act as if God were their boyfriend or girlfriend or something. The woman was a lot like my dad. Which of course is why I was speaking to her. By which I mean listening, and then texting my responses, or sometimes writing my replies on pieces of paper. All of that depending on how I was feeling. Which is something I could get into in more detail, by which I mean why I would text or why I would write. But I probably will not, there being no point.


I talked to her a little bit early on, back then. By then I mean for that first little bit of time after I was home. And by talk I mean she said stuff and I listened. Now I talk to her a bit more often. Which by that I mean we get together more than before, or she will text me. She is nice in that she is not as in my face as much as a psychiatrist or, to be more precise, I should say psychiatrists, but she has the same sort of job or at least I feel that way when we are talking about something that had happened or is happening or, and she worries about this more than me, might someday happen.

But one of the first things she said to me back then, because everyone was confused and did not know what to think about me and of course they had no idea what to say, will always stay with me. Well there are two things, actually. I will talk about both of them because they are related in the same sort of way, even though it is not exactly even.

She wanted me to pray. This was not surprising, given how much she loved church. How she was always at Our Lady of Sorrows. And of course she did not know that I did. By which I mean pray. And so she wanted me to. For whatever reason, although I guess it is because nowadays she comes across most people and most people do not, by which I mean to say pray, she just figured I didn't either.

Prayer might not change God, she told me this one time. But it certainly does change us. By which she meant those of us who do pray.

I wondered how she knew just how to say it that way. Because when I did pray, which was to Mary mostly and was every day, definitely, that was exactly how it was. For real. Not that I felt that God, or Mary, was going to come down and do something. No. It was more like after praying I felt like I was doing everything I possibly could for myself and for other people as well, and also that if something came up and I needed to do something more I would, even if I was unsure how. This, and praying, by which I even mean just the idea of prayer, made me feel like I was smiling.

The, I guess what you would call the actual psychiatrist, was way, way, different. Whenever I met with her, which for a while was twice a week and then, which is now, once a month, she wore this white turtleneck. Well, to be in agreement with myself, I should say it has to be that she has many of them, by which I mean white turtlenecks, because they are all very white, like each one has never been worn before.

Which would be weird, if true. But what do I know? Over this she wears a white jacket, the type you see when actors play doctors on TV. What is weird about her is that she, while definitely a woman, with breasts and all of that, she in other ways did not seem to have a shape. She seems to fall to the ground from her head down, straight through brown corduroys, wool socks, and brown, leather Jesus sandals. The side of her neck and even her jaw is scarred, but not too bad, her skin is not bumpy or anything, there are just these areas that instead of white are bright pink. She is very pretty, only she looks tired by which I mean the sort of tiredness that on some people makes them seem sad. She is also very skinny. By which I mean very. I wondered and I still do wonder if it hurts to hug her. But not enough, by which I mean wonder, to find out.

So for sure I do not think my parents researched Catholic psychiatrists, just the best ones, by which I mean who they thought would be the best shrinks for me to see, and then from those they moved on to select the best doctor, but they got me one. A Catholic psychiatrist I mean to say. As proof, Dr. Anastasio always has on her jacket this small, gold, pin. Of course this pin being a crucifix. And even I can tell it is real gold because of the way it glitters. But even if she did not wear this glittering gold crucifix every day it is obvious that God is important to her and plays this major role in her life decisions.

Many people who hate religion, or who at least go on talking about doing so, act as though every Catholic is just like one of those kids you see on some movie like *Jesus Camp*. Or one of those other documentaries. Like instead of playing with Barbie or handling remote controls we annotate Bibles and juggle snakes. Of course you can take religion too far. But you can take chewing gum too far, too. So please understand. In writing this I am not trying to do anything like that, here.

Which you would call generalize.


One TV show that I do sometimes watch, by which I mean what even I consider regularly, is *Hoarders*. Yes, of course I feel badly for the people on the show. As in the sick people. What you would call the guest stars of each episode. And to be honest I am definitely amazed by that particular sort of insanity, how our minds can be so broken that we feel the medicine for this is collecting the wrists of mannequins and boxes of Peeps from Dollar General.

But this is a good show.

Of course I cannot talk out of one side of my mouth here and one side of my mouth there. Because yeah the sick people on the show are, in the way of TV, just like any other show I have mentioned, used. About this there is no doubt. But everyone else involved. At least the people I can possibly know about, by which I mean there are definitely many people I don't. By which I mean to speak specifically and generally, writers and of course producers. But the hoarder's family members, or many of them, anyway. The psychiatrists. And maybe perhaps and even especially the professional organizers, who, for me, are amazing because I cannot believe we live in a world where these sorts of people are necessary, but, more importantly, how they, over the seasons of the show, become, in time, more like psychiatrists than cleaners and organizers, these really kind and warm guys, although there might be this one woman, too, this is to say those people who, despite the times they get angry and frustrated, are, more than anything, caring, really and truly super people who you can really see have been changed by what they have seen and how what they are doing brings about what it is they see which is and are these good things.

They, by which I mean the psychiatrists but especially the

professional organizers, act so very differently than they did during the show's first season. Before, you could tell, and totally, that it was work. A job. And less a job, and more like work. But over time they change.

There is so much change that over time they become less what they were hired to do and become more what God, and what I, and what you, want people to be. Gentle. Attentive. Aware. Gracious. And because they are gracious, and aware, and attentive, and gentle, so many better things keep on happening. For everyone. And this is so obvious the producers and the writers totally start writing up and producing this side of the show. Which you, by which I mean at least me, know they definitely didn't want to do. And not necessarily most importantly, but what is not the most important thing if not you, by which I mean them, too? So maybe all TV is terrible but using that word, by which I mean terrible, together with the word all, is easy and lazy as well and so this may not be quite fair and necessary. I just don't know.

On Dr. Anistasio's walls there is nothing like you see in the homes of really religious people, the sort that those who post about religion online are called double-dipped. Or, people will say, which is mean but kind of funny, who act like Born Agains on blind dates. No pretty Jesus Christs glossy like models and hanging in fat golden picture frames. No crosses. But she does have this one picture of Mary. You, if you did not spend about fourteen or whatever hours in there a week but instead only passed on through once, you would never have seen it. The picture is set on a small wooden table next to a square box of soft tissues and it never dawned on me until just now, I actually went back to write this, by which I mean to add this part in, that maybe she puts out the picture of Mary before I come and then takes it off when I leave, by which I mean that this picture is put there just for me. I do not know. But this could be. The picture looks like this: The picture is a portrait. The background is brown, what kids on their phones would call sepia and it gets even browner at the edges like one of those old-time Wanted posters. And it is one of those images that looks like a photograph of a painting. Mary is young but older-looking than a high school student. She is pretty but this is because of how simple she appears. Dressed like a nun she has a lot of darker blue on, but her eyes are the bright subdued blue of those outside Christmas lights. Her cheeks and lips are red. She is wearing her crown of twelve stars which, if you want to, you can google to find out what that means. She smiles like the Mona Lisa. And while I try not to stare at the picture because I do not want to be asked questions about Mary or talk more about her than I already have, or will, I do think I can see the source, by which I mean meaning, which of course means life-giving and even more important to me this purifying element and this, the source, is something I think I always see.

Again, I understand if you do not believe me. And of course this is not interesting enough for *Dry The Rain* because if the story is about anything it really is more about Him than me. Or if it is about me it is about how I react to Him. Which of course I get. I do not think that is crazy. But when we met and when we meet I do not speak. She, which is to say Dr. Anastasio, thinks that she is being cool and making friends with me by not talking either, by which I mean in terms of with her mouth speaking but instead texting. And we carry on talking in this particular way which is fine but pretty unremarkable to me. I do not mind seeing her because it is something to do and more important than this I know it makes my mom happy. And there are times when I do think she is helping. Though I could not exactly say how.

She asks me a lot about my dreams and while of course I have them, because who does not, these what I consider mind movies, these mind movies I consider secrets about myself, things I tell myself that I promised never to tell anyone, I say, by which I mean type, I can't remember. Although what she has to say about dreams is definitely interesting and sometimes useful and I do wonder if I should tell her more. Because I do use that to help me, by which I mean what she says.

The cameras. Some detective or cop sold at least some of them, by which I of course mean the videos, by which I mean the footage, to MovieTrap. Or at least someone let some of the producers and then let some of the writers who made *Dry The Rain* watch them and take down notes. I have heard that while they do not use, which by that I mean actually show His tapes of me, the producers and the writers who made and are still making *Dry The Rain*, which by this I mean they do edit, or whatever, between showing episodes through Movietrap and on TV, they do this thing where they basically create the film of me exactly as it would be if Imogen was down in my cellar instead of me. As in this what you would call frame by frame thing. Because of this, this is one reason why Imogen even more so than the show itself is up for all sorts of awards. Remarkable, is what everyone calls her acting, when she moves around exactly like I do, either talking to herself or not saying a thing when it got to that point for me. But I am sure she never had to act out any of the really hard things, there being a particular method to that sort of thing. But that is another story.

.  .  .

He of course knew I was exercising. But as I have already said He did not mind me exercising. By which I mean He liked me exercising, how it made my body look. Which even I knew was good. What I did, aside from sit-ups and pushups, was position myself underneath my mattress, with my blankets and pillows placed directly in one spot, the cellar floor hard and cold beneath my bottom and back and skull and I used my mattress like a huge weight. In the beginning I could only push it up and down a couple of times. But I do think all of you would believe that I got strong. As you of course know and absolutely believe, this is the part that Imogen Appelton says was her favorite part about me. By which I mean playing me. Or should I say Mallory. Getting fit. She said she never knew how much fun exercising could be. That, and that she did not even really have to watch out that much for what she was eating, because of her metabolism or something.

Once I was out of my chains I knew I would not even need something sharp like the scissors, that because He was so old and not only was I so strong I was so filled with anger and something I feel but cannot name that it would not be a fair fight. But there was a lot about Him that I did not know. So much to be exact. So I knew that I needed to wait. I just needed to get every angle I could get. Which for a while, by which I mean quite some time, meant I got stronger, and then stronger.

Here is how I killed Him. Like I said I have not seen it. How they show and are showing me on *Dry The Rain*. You have not seen this either. But you will. And how I have no interest in any of that, either.

For you watching at home this will be Episode Nine, I

think, *Kill Him Until He Dies*, which is something I did say, and which of course has not yet played on TV. If that is not about this then again I am confused by what they, by which I mean the producers and the writers, are up to. Which would not be the first time. From what I have heard, by which I mean read, because this episode has not been on TV yet, but of course people have seen the entire thing, the producers sharing it with all these famous and popular writers and producers who talk about what is worth watching, who then share it with what I think you would call surreptitiously with what I know you call influencers, so that people like you will turn on and watch, they show it mostly right.

This is what I had been thinking during a lot of my time down there. By which I mean my cellar. There will not be much time. I will not fail. It will happen when I am cutting my hair. I don't speak so I need to be ready to scream. I need to train myself how to use what you, at least if you are a teacher, or a person who trains people in self-defense, call tactical profanity. You will kill Him until He is dead. Until He dies. This is what I tell myself. By which I mean told myself. Again and again. Over and over.

For one week before it was time to cut my hair I was directed to act moody. By which I mean by Mary. By which I do not mean me being not rude or refusing Him in any way because I am not insane. I mean, why go ahead and get myself ready to kill Him, only to have Him beat me senseless. Or worse. But I will not be pleasant. You think you would never act pleasant towards a Man who hurts you this way, by now Him coming up with different ways to rape and sodomize me as if thinking His way through Wordle. Or as if playing a game of Tetris, to speak of this more accurately. You would tell your best friend, Screw him and some of you would type, Fuck that. You would say that you would have resisted. Fought back. Or that you would rather be dead. That, Hell no, there is no way. I do know this is hard to believe. After all, you are basing your opinion from what you have seen from what they show you on other shows. I can certainly say and tell you that I did not. By which I mean have anything. By which I mean I was not based.

This will confuse Him, I knew, me acting moody, because I am always good and always had been. Of course He never got to liking me liking me, but I do think He found me surprising. I am sure other girls did other interesting things. Especially because in being killed so quickly they had time to do things I did not. By which I mean to react. To really and totally freak out. And I am sure He found that fascinating. But I was for sure no doubt around Him the longest and I did all sorts of things all of the time and even more importantly I had time to do these things. Which is of course much different from what I just said. About time, I mean. And this, instead of being pretty or beautiful, or surprising Him and being interesting, is something I can be proud of because doing things a lot of different ways, by which I mean other than I thought and considered to do them, would have been easy and would have gotten me killed. Or worse.

So, I told myself. When I have the scissors I am going to twist a wad of my hair and cut it in half and throw my hair across the cellar and then when He is looking at my hair, the handful clump I just threw, I am going to scream and stab my mattress. Now this is important because He will not think that the scissors are in my hand. He will think that His scissors are in the mattress. And of all the things He cared about, me not speaking, by which I mean remaining totally silent, was not one of them. So the sound of my voice, I knew, would shock Him.

This is also important. He only has two emotions. And they flip as quickly as a bird sings. In His rage He will attack me. Even He will not know why He is attacking me, just that He has to, which will make this plan work even way more in my favor. He will have a fist raised to punch me in the nose which He knows will completely stun me. This is when I will, just before He gets to me, grab the scissors from the mattress and jump and stick His scissors into His face and then when He, with His hands makes for His face, I will remove the scissors and plunge His scissors into His neck.

And then I will pummel His nose and His teeth until He is drowning on His blood and choking on His broken teeth.

And I will smash Him with my chain.

And I will butt Him with my head.

And then I will plant my hands behind me as best as possible and from on top of my mattress like a horse or maybe a donkey I will kick Him with both feet, the sensors on my chains blinking and blinking and blinking.

I know, I know, some of you are already saying. Yeah right.

And I do understand your position. Your point of view. Because there is a problem. The only problem with my plan is that I am chained. And as I have said He is perfectly careful. He of course never thinks I have a chance. But still. Whenever He comes down to be with me He never brings keys. Never.

So, some of you might think and type. That is all fine and good, me killing Him, but why? Only to die, starving to death, or from dehydration, chained to a wall like my famous horse or donkey.

But to unlock myself?

You see, of course I have been provided a way.

Episode Six, *Civil Arts*, one of the episodes that I did,

when I had the chance, watch most of, because I really like what I did here, gives you some sort of clue. But that is totally inaccurate by the way. By which of course I mean what you will see in that episode. Still. That part was interesting for me to remember. To talk to the producers and the writers about.

You want to know what He looks like. At first, that's all anyone cared about. Even after the first picture was on TV, and then of course the Internet, whenever that was, that wasn't enough. As if it matters. As if Him looking like a high school English teacher or a used, by which I now know to say pre-owned car salesman, makes any sort of difference. But this is the truth. While I could describe His penis to a police sketch artist so great the picture would get fingered in a lineup, I did not see His face much. I do not think there is a major reason for this. It just is. As in if you think about it we did not often hang out together, and when He was around me I just did not want to look at Him. Also, and when I could have my body, by which I mean my face, I was not usually in the best position to do so. Look at Him, I mean to say.

But sure. Of course I know what He looks like. The man in the movie, by which I mean the famous actor from that one movie about the monkeys, is pretty close. By which I mean when it comes to looking like Him. But even with makeup I do not think there is just quite any way to get another person looking just like Him. There are two reasons for this. Well, those and this one other which is because so much of what He looked like came about because of who He is. But maybe if you try this. This could work.

Picture your best friend's grandfather. Now, give him curly white hair, hair that is sort of puffy, like a cotton ball. Now, picture that his white hair is the white of a used cigarette filter. Now, picture one of those games they give little kids when they are little. That little board with the picture of the smiling bald man covered in plastic and all those little bits of magnets cut up like clipped hair that little kids can move around with that little red plastic stick with a magnet at the end. So you could give that white man hair. Now, turn that into Him and give Him one of those big noses, a nose like some broken beak, all blue with veins and gross with huge black pores. Now, imagine that His face is very red. Like the inside of His face got sunburned, red. Now, think it is like there is a fishhook buried in the side of His face and that someone is reeling Him in. I never knew if it was a scar, or if He was born that way, like maybe He got squished or somehow cut up when He was coming out of whatever His mother was, but it was not possible to think that He had ever lived one day in His life without His face all yanked-back looking. Or you could sort of picture Santa Claus, dressed up as a clown, having a stroke while standing on top of an earthquake. Like I said, it is difficult.


It was my last Christmas with Him that I was given the dress the producers had the costume designers make a copy of for *Dry The Rain*. At least I think so. That, and He gave me a pack of underwear, or what men love to call panties, a pack of black socks, a red hooded sweatshirt, and rain boots. These were things that I had grown out of a long time ago, and when I was asked about this a man from the FBI, I think, asked me if I wanted to know what he thought.

About what? I had asked him.

About why he gave you those particular items.

His question is basically the only question I have ever been asked that ever surprised me, because while I did not think He got me presents, in a Christmas way, I think He gave them to me around Christmas because it was that time of year and He just did so out of habit or something. Without even thinking about what He was doing. And like I said or at least suggested I was growing really tall and nothing fit at all.

Of course you are saying How could I know it was Christmas, and of course I do not know for sure, but I think it was Christmas because the cellar had been much colder and a week before it had snowed and it was just this feeling I had. It was definitely that time of year based on what I saw through my window, and based on the number of times I had to recently dry the rain. Which is to say not many. The pine trees were outlined in snow and the birds were bright brown and red against the white. I could not remember the last time I had been let out to dry the rain. But there was more to it than that. I figured it had to do with His job or something, but He was for sure and more than just occasionally wearing red and green.

You're probably right that it was Christmas before that, the man who I thought was an FBI agent said. But, and he spoke slowly like most people did, especially back then, just to make sure that his words were not in any way bothering me while at the same time making sure I understood. Because some people did and still do think I am dumb. To which I can only say you can and will draw your own conclusions, and, like most people, or, maybe to be more exact, like most little kids, you just do not draw well.

But you had long outgrown what you were at the time wearing, the man who I thought was from the FBI said. Correct?

I nodded.

Well, going back one Christmas, when it would be natural for an older man to be purchasing items of clothing for a young woman, at least as normal as something like that gets, and through maybe some point in time before Thanksgiving. He was purchasing these items. The FBI had figured that out. By looking at His bank records. In His mind shopping then was a precaution to make sure He remained undetected. He was that careful. That caring.

He, the FBI guy, must have thought what was on my face looked upset. This was not true. I was just really surprised to be spoken to that way because no one ever told me anything that I considered interesting. Or that I did not know. Especially anything at all about Him. And even more especially than that, anything that had to do with stuff that He had done to me.

I say that, the FBI guy said, not for any reason other than to underscore that your survival. Your escape. From a man like him. It really is something remarkable. And that is just the truth.


And so yeah. Maybe so. Or I guess of course maybe not. By which I mean about this being remarkable. What I do know is that winters were the worst. Of course there was nothing. The Earth was so much uglier, by which I mean unless it snowed, and it never snowed except for occasionally, and the trees without their leaves looked like nature was smiling and had this face full of cavities. His backyard and even His fence lost all of its color and what you would call dimension. And the sky was low and gray. Me looking through that very thick glass of my window with what you would call deep pockets of privity. Me passing through that very particular existence, by which I mean it was like I felt not like a minute or a second hand but the screw that holds them there, centered inside of their clock.

Also with the winter, too. First, like I sort of got at before, it rarely rained. And I only dry the rain. None of the drying I had to do had to do with melted snow. So that just meant unless I was being raped or sodomized or was learning something new and was paying attention to what He was saying while he made His points with ballpoint pens or paper clips, it was just me and the chain. And second, if it did rain, the ground was so cold that drying the grass hurt. This was easier to do, by which I mean dry the rain, because the ground was frozen. But still. It hurt.

But anything different was, if fun is not the right word, well then certainly the feeling right next to it. My dress was white and somehow it fit me perfectly. It had long sleeves, deep pockets, and when I was standing it came down to my ankles. I did not dream I was a fairy queen or anything, but it was dreamy being what you and your friends call comfy. The cellar was clean, this being one of the first things He taught me with a syringe from one of those dessert decorating sets, and I could use the sink and soap as often as I liked, so, given there was not much to do being this quite terrible and literal thing, I washed my socks and underwear regularly, leaving them on the edge of the sink to dry. I washed my dress only when necessary. I did this an hour or two before bed. Because He of course took all my old clothing, I wrung the dress dry, hung it across the sink and in my underwear and socks wrapped myself in my blankets and went to sleep.

Of course many times me falling asleep was not possible. I knew that somewhere, out there, by which I mean both beyond and across His backyard the wind had risen. That the wind was strong enough to smash and fall apart against the side of His house because I could see dust like snow falling from the ceiling. And I would sit up and wipe my mouth with the back of my hand. Standing, I would turn on the faucet and sip water from my sink. I would look out my window.

The sky would be clear and the moon would be huge. The moonlight a sort of magic making things bright or other spots dark and how it did not matter what I believed. I did not know how and I still do not know how but the moon would seem so thin. Like how when you leave a glass of water on a piece of paper the paper becomes thin and it is simple to poke your finger in, by which I mean through. I heard nothing.

One thing I did know was that out there, through the glass, there was sound. Birds hidden in their nests were singing, by which I mean calling, their crazed calls maybe attracting mates or possibly defining territories or to be honest I am not sure what all birds do, or were doing, by which I mean back then. Beneath this noise some sound that seemed far away, but could not be, and this would be something I could not name and would be so much different from what it was like early in the morning, outside, life and the world fresh with early morning urgency that it did not matter who created what.

During this time and times like these I had little control over what you would consider my emotions, and I would not so much have them, by which I mean they would have me. As sad as I was when my grandma died, nothing quite bothered me so much as when my cat Solomon died. I thought about that sometimes. If not often.

I have no idea why, but I was down near the creek by our home. It had not rained in a long time and the ground was very dry and there were deep cracks. Solomon was very dead, by which I mean when I saw him I stopped moving and breathing. He did not seem hurt but somehow he was very, very, skinny and one of his eyes was missing. Ants were crawling in and out of the hole. There were so many ants that even though they were moving they, all together, seemed still and because of how hard their bodies were, black like shells on M&Ms, they made this sort of mirror that reflected the sun. I screamed and then even though I felt that it was wrong I brought him home.

My Aunt and Uncle Billy were visiting and they were sitting on the deck with my parents when I came running through our backyard carrying a dead cat. My mom's first instinct was to be a mom which meant that she wanted to make sure I was okay and then after that to make sure I stayed okay, which of course meant taking Solomon, who of course could have died from anything, away from me. Like a teardrop, by which I mean how it, a tear, can form in your eye and for a moment bubble before falling, I felt like that as my mom took the cat and I sort of slid to the ground on my knees.

I do not remember much other than a lot of chaos and that I would not take a shower until Solomon was buried which my mom said could wait until later and my dad said could wait until later and my aunt said that she was sorry and that Solomon would be okay and that I needed to listen to my mom, too. Uncle Billy left and returned carrying a shovel and told me to jump in the pool and he looked at my mom and I think she must have nodded or something because even though I did not know what was happening exactly, whenever I was confused Uncle Billy did not try and make me understand he simply acted, by which I mean did something about whatever was going on.

I am not saying Uncle Billy is like this religious figure or anything like that but, like Mary, he was quite quiet and was happier when things were calm and cool. I slid out of my shorts and top and jumped into our pool. I sort of spun around in place until I saw Uncle Billy. He had Solomon scooped up on the end of the shovel and he was walking back towards the creek and then he stopped by what he knew was my favorite tree. I swam to the far end of the pool, this would be the deep end, and I sort of perched there with my arms on the wooden deck, watching. He turned to me and I knew what he meant and I nodded. A million gnats were gathering around my head and when they got to be too much I would duck under the water. And then I would come back up again.

The big thing about Uncle Billy was that more than anything and any other person I had ever known he was just patient not just with people, but the world. He found it easy to smile. When there were people around and if it got quiet people got into these races to make sure that something was being said. There was for them, even the people I liked, nothing easy about insignificance. This is what made Uncle Billy so simple to be around. He did not make anything difficult to understand. If a person wanted to talk he would listen to what they had to say, but for him conversations were like things. By which I mean like a vase was a vase because it held flowers. An ashtray was an ashtray because it held ashes. Books were sure of course things you could read, but a book was something that could just be something that held pages of words, too. This is how it was. That is how it would forever be. If he could have his way he would erase so much everything. Later that night, after everyone had gone back inside after trying to make me feel better, he stepped onto the deck.

I was up much later than usual. While warm, change was coming, summer turning into a season that I would, until I killed Him, never again have free. But of course I was only thinking about my cat. And not even that. It was like how later on it would be like how things were like with Him, by which I mean I was just feeling. While of course it would be different, by which I mean what I saw from His backyard, the pine trees that more yes than less made up what we considered the end of our backyard, because beyond that was the creek and what most people called The Woods, what I was looking at was not all that different. They were, by which I mean the trees, like these tall black shapes black against a dark blue sky. I would have a thought and it would fall away and I would wonder where it went, and I would realize that wondering about that was my thought, and then I would realize I was thinking about that, and then about that, and I must have looked funny because Uncle Billy started to laugh. He asked me if I wanted to hear a cool story. I did.

He told me this story about how trees communicate. That, for example, acacias call out to other acacias, warning of the presence of nearby giraffes, grazing. I liked his story, which I do not remember, but I do remember him going on and into greater, by which I mean more, detail. I forget that, by which I mean those details, too. But that is not important. Recalling him telling, feeling the time he took is what I count, those are the moments I can experience and measure.

While I loved Uncle Billy's stories, what I most liked was not what they made me think. Because he gave me all of this stuff to consider, he did not put me under any pressure to what you or my psychiatrists would call process, let alone share back. If I had what you or my psychiatrist would call a sentiment, or opinion, sure, Uncle Billy would be interested to hear what I had to say, by which I mean my opinion, or sentiment, but these, by which I mean opinions, were nothing he expected me to have. Let alone defend or, like I have said, even come up with. This is something that I do hope all of you have in your lives. By which I mean your version of Uncle Billy. Just so that you can have silence. Because so long as we are living and alive nothing is permanent.


So with trees then, so like humans. I do not know how I knew these things, and while I do think it is interesting that one tree warns a sister or brother tree that their leaves are about to be eaten, it was not as though a tree could really do anything, by which I mean to defend itself. Maybe, I was thinking, or maybe I am just having this thought now, but maybe in like one million years these trees through, say, evolution, would find some way to make themselves weapons, by which I mean they could use their branches like hands to strangle giraffes or something. Or maybe they could become poisonous and like snakes create venom not so that they could bite animals, but so that, if bitten, by which I mean their leaves, the animals doing the biting would suffer. But until then all that trees could do was scream to one another, and this as loudly as dog whistles.


I had not been prepared for sadness, by which I mean the sort associated with loss, and only Uncle Billy seemed to understand this. The world, by which I mean nature, controlled our reality, and he let me have my emotions. He did not try to talk them away. I did not know what to feel, and in time, as he remained more and more quiet, I got less and less confused. Then he said something funny. And he did not expect me to laugh. Or to smile. I just did.

.  .  .

I do not go now, but when I was little, and had no say in things, my parents took me to church. Our Lady of Sorrows. My dad, more than my mom, believed in God. I know that now. My mom did not mind mass, but now, when I think back, I can see my mom and her eyes were always open, not because she did not want to miss something, but because I am just sure she did not really believe in anything and she was more interested in what there was to see.

Church, by which I mean being involved, was a very social thing, and she was always ready to talk, she was always wanting to talk and she was the church's, by which I mean Our Lady of Sorrows, biggest celebrity so that meant a lot of talking. She was popular. And of course she was what many of you call hot. This meant that we were popular. But she never sang the hymns. I think the music irritated her. This was not personal or anything. It was just that, for my mom, who loved and loves music, the playing was far from sounding professional. Nowadays my mom never talks about church, but she will say stuff about not liking something because it is country, R&B, or folk, and Church music, at least to me, is country, R&B, and it is, of course, folk.

My dad did not sing, either, but that is because he has always been sort of quiet and shy. But he always opened the hymnal and followed along reading as the woman at the lectern sang and it was obvious that he was, in his mind, singing, thinking about the words, while my mom was listening to the music, enjoying, or at least trying to appreciate, the sounds.


It is difficult to write about my dad. It was horrible watching him lose his power to speak, to see like one of those framed pictures of Mary how sad his eyes were. I am trying now to remember the last conversation, by which I mean just the last things we said to one another before He stole me, and of course it is not possible to remember. But I am sure he does. I know he plays those words over and over. It is not true what people think about death. We have more than this one life to lose.

Why? I once heard him say this to my mom.

I do not know what they were talking about. I know that me going missing and what he must have imagined and is left living imagining, him being a guy and all, has ruined huge parts of him. Like me, he is not the same. What my mom said does not make sense to me now, but I like, when I am alone and thinking, working out what it means. She said, by which I mean to my father, It's happening because it's happening. The why is the is.

How, then, can a child, like a flower pressed between two pages in a book, become to her father a memory of something worth preserving? Something not so easily destroyed. A girl strong as a weed, not easily destroyed no matter if pulled apart petal by petal from stem and pistil, her dad left holding the artifact petrified, feeling that, once opened, left unpreserved, the flower will flit and flake and fall to the ground until all that remains is the impression on the paper, that extra blown out space within the pages of the book.

I just don't know.

Not being a woman he does not know that while it is bad, it is not nearly as bad, by which I mean what is leftover, from what men think they do to us.

Even Him.

Not if you do not let them. This is because we just do not care that much about you. Well I guess I should only speak for myself, and this is to say I don't. By which I mean care about Him.

I would not be here if I did. Even if I was here, I would be there. There is no way he, which is to say my dad, can understand that I really am okay, and it is only for him, and because of this, that I feel sadness.


He is the kind of person to have known that I am dead. I am sure that in time my mom gave up hope, I mean she is just way too smart to have, knowing all of the statistics, spent time believing I was alive and somehow well and living, but that did not mean she doubted I could have still been alive. My dad though. Even now, as time goes on, I catch him looking at me like I am a ghost.


I have never wanted to go fishing. At least not really. I love going fishing, as in I love being near the water and being out on a boat, in this wonderful ship out there on top of the water. Doing that, being on top of the water, is something that really does amaze and will never stop amazing me. To point at a fact, you will see this by the end of this story. The way that my body feels different and the way that moving feels different. The way that the air feels different and the way that smelling tastes different. And I also love, and always will love, being with the man who loves fishing most, my Uncle Billy.

But I never want to catch a fish. The first time I caught a fish was horrifying. This was on my very first ever cast, me catching my first fish. It is because of this fact that I remember what happened so much and so very brightly. I can still feel it, by which I mean that fish taking the lure, much more than anything He ever did to me and my body. I wished

I never caught another fish again, but of course I did. That being the point of fishing even if you are not trying, and even if you are praying to, with your lure, miss.

I was of course with my uncle. What I loved most about him was that he rarely spoke. And he would never say anything at all until I said something. Then he would smile and carry on as if we had been having this important and interesting conversation for hours. He was the first person I made myself not think about when He stole me, and by that I mean of course I knew it would be impossible not to ever think about my mom and my dad.

We were not at the shore but at a lake house. There are lakes all over Virginia, but this was in West Virginia. There is one picture from this time during the introduction of *Dry The Rain*. It is that one picture of me smiling and holding the fishing pole. Pretty much seconds after that picture was taken I followed my uncle to the dock. The dock was way long and I was excited, thinking I wanted to catch this fish. The lake was huge, and all around us were woods. The water was totally and completely calm, it was more like a pond. The sky was blue.

Like I said I am tall and was tall for my age. If I did not say this before I should have. I was and am really quite athletic. Sports for the sake of competing, I was too young for that when He stole me. But I was lucky in that I just had fun ice skating or playing ping-pong. Playing tee-ball and soccer. So after my uncle showed me what to do I just went and did it.

My lure went sailing far overhead and the feeling was thrilling. I could feel the weight of the hook, which was part of this fake looking fish, leading the line for what felt like forever. And then when the lure hit the water it was just like that. A fish attacked the lure. And I felt not the pole or the lure or the string or even myself but just this crazy and what I would call dead heavy movement of the fish. There is no real way to describe it, how I knew that the animal had made a mistake and was in fear and I do not want to try. Which is to say I do not want to think of a way to find the words to describe that feeling. Or even worse what I was knowing. I never saw that one, this first fish. This is because what I did was drop the pole and I turned and ran and kept running down the deck.

Because of Him so much of my dad is dead. Even though I am back home and alive and he is happy he is still filled with so much great sadness. I have no idea what my mom and my dad went through and I do not ask them and I do not want to guess. But this I can tell you. Do not believe one minute of what you see on *Dry The Rain* because one deal my parents made was that if I provided the producers and the writers with information they would not. Talk, this is to say. I think they just figured I would watch the show and they did not want to make me feel any worse. So everything about them is made up from stories told by other people based on their memories of what my mom and dad had been doing and of course made bigger and more fantastic by the producers and by the writers.

My dad, who on the show is played by Dave Abrahams, who is mostly a voice actor because his voice is so great and my dad is not a big part of the story on TV, does not believe in God. At least I do not think so. I mean I think he does, but he does so in his way, which is not like I do, which of course involves Mary and is much more complicated and does involve those things that so many of you and other people have problems with.


My dad does not go to church, he goes to mass. There is a difference. And he does not go to mass just because, like me, he has been going ever since he was a baby, taken by his parents. He goes because he wants to. Because he is willing. Once, when I was meeting with my mom's friend and she was talking about God, she said that she always found it strange how people would say God didn't exist, or they, which is to say these people, didn't believe in God because what kind of God would allow such terrible things to happen. By which these people meant to them. And to other good people on planet Earth. And, as far as that goes, to the planet Earth itself. But that, she had said, was wrong. When they spoke this way, she said, it meant, if you followed their words logically, that there had to be a God who could exist only to allow good things to happen. To people. And to planet Earth. But God is not conditional, she said. To say there is no God because Evil exists is the exact same thing as saying that God does exist. She did not say this exactly like that, but mainly. And she said so softly. And gently. Just like it made all this perfect sense. And it does. It did.


My going and talking about my dad though. Well, he is way too full of common sense to believe in that stuff of the Church that makes the Church so old-fashioned and what you could even say sick to so many people. And I am not even getting close to something as easy as The Scandal. Or like his position on something like abortion. To get at this, by which I mean his position on abortion, is to say that he knows what he would do, but that this is easy for him to say because he would never have to do anything. He, personally, is against it. By which I mean abortion. I am sure of this and I know because I heard him talking when I first got home, he of course having no idea that I was around hearing. What he had said was that even if they had found me pregnant or if it turned out I was pregnant, he, which is to say my dad, would not have wanted me to kill it. His baby made by me, as well, that is to say. That he really believed that they would be killing more of me than Him, and by that I know he was talking about two different things.

Because babies do not and cannot grow inside his body he does not believe, as much as he hates the idea of hacking up babies into parts and sucking babies' parts through vacuum cleaners, that the Church, or the government, should have a say in what people do with their bodies. The idea that you cannot wear a condom? Dumb. He is more the kind of person to get frustrated that having a baby, as in literally having it, inside of you for however long and then come out of you, is something that not only makes men and women different, but separates us, which he feels divides us, and he also I know for a fact is sad that he, because he is a man, cannot have a baby, personally. As in he wishes both men and women could have babies. Because he would really like to have one. That is how amazing he thinks babies are. And, if you were to ask me, that is the main reason he thinks there are so many problems, generally. Because the world does not like or enjoy differences. And when it comes to men and women it does not get any more different than this.

I know what many of you are saying. Even if you believe me when I say my dad would have wanted me to have and deliver my rape baby, how would I know this for real and for sure. People say a lot of things, some of you say. Well I do not know what to tell you other than I am and always have been around my parents a lot and I listen to what they say and also to what they do not say. And this. I understand. I do not think it is easy being you any more than I know it is tough being me.

In order to be Catholic, and not go to Hell, you need to believe that when the priest prays over the bread and the wine this, by which I mean what you simply think is bread and wine, actually, as in literally, turns into the body and blood of Jesus. And so people will make lame puns, like saying they find that doctrine difficult to swallow. Or bad jokes, like, if at a Catholic wedding saying, I'll have to pass. I'm vegetarian.

I understand.

This is because it is not cool.

It is like admitting that you are not cool, that you are not in control and there is for so many of you nothing more important than being cooler and more in control than not even your friends but your idea of and how it is you think of yourself. I have not been back to school for anything more than some meetings that, according to my mom and dad, were required by the law, but I do have some homeschool friends, which by that I mean people my age who I more yes than less trust, who I talk to online, who as kids were not allowed to watch much TV, let alone shows like *Dry The Rain*, and what they all have in common is that they are at least somewhat into God, if not quite very, which, while of course it is a good thing, is also kind of a bad thing both for home-schooling and for God, if you know what I mean.

.   .   .

The rest of them, like kids I see at the Endwell Mall the every so often I go there with my mom, these kids have no faith at all, they are totally messed up. I see this most at the food court. Of course, at first, my mom never left my side. But she tried not to totally freak out all the time, and would let me stand hipshot against a metal table, an object looking just like a white mushroom, surrounded by four smaller, red mushrooms, drinking from a cup of soda without a lid or a straw because my mom told me what plastic and straws are doing to the planet and I believe her.

It is easy to remember, then. Standing there I hear all these electronic bloops and bleeps escaping from the Endwell Arcade, which is next to Endwell Pizza, and even though I know the arcade has kids in it, from where I stand, by which I mean from where I look, all I see is a dark box and, maybe, every once in a while, these slow-moving shapes, and I see illuminated neon green and bug-zapper blue these very serious faces. Inside, and it is hard not to think of my sink from His cellar, light from I guess what you would call one of those claw cranes fills with stuffed cartoon characters I am still catching up on and pointless rubber balls, and way in the back when they shoot enough and there is light from the game's huge screen I watch a few teens holding toy weapons, methodically blasting away what I think are these oversized aliens. Or maybe they are robots. Or humans. Anyways. I do not get it. Standing around in the dark killing things does not seem fun.

There were times, and being at the food court was one of them, when I had trouble concentrating, by which I mean I just could not think well. At all. To begin with, there were so many boys. Some were angular, really skinny and straight and they reminded me of the problems I was looking at in math, and those boys wore glasses and small tee shirts. Most, though, were overweight, by which I mean, and not to be mean, fat. By which I mean you could push them with a pin and they would pop. In their long mesh shorts, tight t-shirts, white socks, and dirty sneakers, they looked used, dusty, and not at all happy.

This, for sure, by which I mean boys, was all so very confusing.


People hate Roman Catholicism. And there are plenty of reasons to hate religion, any religion, without adding bad priests to what I think of as a math problem. But there are more reasons to love them. Priests and religions, I mean. And saying that all priests are pedophiles is just like saying all men are like Him. Or that all TV is like *Dry The Rain*. And most priests and most men just are not. And there is nothing on TV like *Dry The Rain*. This is something that I do believe. And there are good shows to watch as well. This is also something I believe. And were I to be happy about anything, it would be, along with some other things, that I hold these beliefs.


On *Dry The Rain* my mom is acted by the rapper $ister, Brother. Like my dad, my mom does not have a big part in the show, and so I think picking an actor who has never really acted before is sort of like how really big bands, or bands at those festivals so popular nowadays, will have smaller, really popular bands, even if they are only really popular for this one small group of people, play before them, this being a sort of way to get more people who ordinarily would not be watching to get them in front of their TVs watching. Or, of course, buying tickets to the festivals. And of course there were my parents and my uncle, but aside from them I missed music more than anything.

There are a few ways, but music is the biggest way how I know God exists. Before that morning He got me over to His van and stole me, I already loved music more than I cared about most human beings. This, more than anything, explains why I was alone, riding my bike in the church parking lot, near that one corner of the woods, airpods in, totally not concerned about some man and His van. Every day and every week I just grew so tired of people, especially girls and very much the ones my age, these little human beings so full of ideas and who used words to create sentences they would never say if their parents or a teacher was around. I really did not know what they had to do with me.

Why aren't you looking at me? was what everything sounded like. Don't you want to know what I think?

No, I wanted to scream. Can't you see that I already know?

It was not any more personal than who I was as a person.

The only thing I loved more than music were the few people who, by being, played the sort of music that, like what you heard from birds, filled me not so much with peace and feeling really good and calm, but the very big and over-whelming sense that here, on planet Earth, there was so much more than me and that because of this there were people, maybe not many, but enough, who I was made to meet. Like a favorite singer once said:  If music was warm, these musicians were my suns. Well, at least sort of. By which I mean that is sort of what the singer said.

Me, I would never make music. I never wanted music to be something I had to think about and to work at. I never wanted to risk taking anything away from what it was like to have music wash over and then come into me. But I did know that I would form a human note. It was clear that I, along with some others, would help to create a beautiful sound. I have not been wrong about that.

I do not know if you have yet seen the different episodes of *Dry The Rain* that have been on TV, and while it does not matter I am pretty sure that many of you have. Those who care about me. And those who just want something to watch. To see. But in case you have not. Spoiler Alert. It turns out that He worked for a Toyota dealership, at least I think so, it was something to do with cars, by which I mean what He did for a job is He worked at a place where it is that people who own lots of new cars sell them, which of course means they sell trucks and vans as well and this is some point of His life and my ordeal that they let out early on. They let this part out pretty early on because they did have to show a lot of Him throughout all of the series but could not just keep showing Him in His house doing whatever it is they thought He would be doing. They wanted to make Him look normal. Which in my opinion was a pretty smart decision because it is impossible to make anything up. And this allows the producers and the writers to make Him look that much more human. By which I mean He had friends and coworkers and all of that. And they could get a lot of truth from His friends and coworkers for really cheap as well, everybody willing to talk and wanting to say they were a part of something other than themselves. As if that is such a bad thing to be.

All that they, by which I mean the producers and the writers, knew for sure is part of what He did to me. And I only told them some of the things and I told them the particularly gross stuff because it was fun watching them trying to listen and not act like they should, which is to say grossed out and horrified, and it was not as though they could show those, by which I mean the very worst things. Or even really hint at them repeatedly. Even MovieTrap has its limits. Like the stuff with the ant traps. Or that period of time with the jelly donuts. Otherwise the show, while it might have been made and put on TV, would not have been seen by as many people. And by that I mean the younger kids, like teens, kids not much younger than me, who have parents who still care and watch out for what they watch on their TVs and their devices and of course that would not have been good because of course and obviously the producers wanted as many people as possible watching and that includes you and you know what I mean when I say me.

I am not sure I would have thought of this. But I do believe this. That it is simply impossible to just make something up that no one has ever before seen. The reason for that is because of this one program, I do not know if it was real or not, but the idea is real and I read about it in a short story. Here. I will copy the part I am talking about.

*A dozen artists are directed to draw, based on belief or speculation, an alien. The artists have one hour, and work secretly, in private studios, off camera. When their time is up, the drawings are set on easels, and the easels are placed on four steel risers, the aliens arranged like members of a studio audience. Using a laser pointer to highlight googly single eyes, webbed, amorphous hands, squat bellies, and ears hanging from tentacles, the host asks what each drawing has in common.*

*"You're unsure, aren't you?" the host says. "Well, how about this. Every artist," the man explains, smiling at the TV audience. "All of our guests relied on human, and animal, attributes." He points his space-age laser and highlights too-thin nose slits, crinkly fingers, moony eyelids, and incongruous, stumpy teeth. "This isn't to insult. This isn't to disparage our wonderfully gifted artists. No! Not at all." He smiles. "This is because it is impossible to conceive of the inconceivable. Nothing is unprecedented. Nothing." He rocks back and forth on his heels. "Is new under the sun."*

I cannot remember who wrote it, my memory is not that great, but I have read many of her stories. She is one person I definitely would love to write about me. Because she knows. I am not new, or different, just because I was stolen.

Anyways, by now you have probably guessed at least some of how I managed to escape. And yes, you are correct. You are not right, because there is totally this difference, but you are not wrong, or completely incorrect. And if I think to do so, by which I mean if I want to, I will explain how and what this has to do with the birds, especially those birds I now, thanks to what I want to be part of my profession, can name. The birds that, like sign language, sing every night. The birds, so smart, who sing in the morning because the air is different and allows their songs to travel as far as possible, and so who every morning sing. But that might be giving you, even those of you I am sure I can like, just a little bit too much. So, no. I will not write about those birds. Or if I do, maybe just the one.

. . .

What happened and who knows when, other than it was not stupid Episode Seven, *Nocturnal Emission*, is that I, over the course of time, eventually, just because life becomes life, began to sleep. By which I mean I began to sleep without waking up remembering my dreams. And by this I mean in any way at all.

Before that I never woke up fully rested and so I always felt confused and weak, what you would call disoriented. This is because my dreams, at least one or two a night, were terrible things. They were worse than what you consider nightmares because they were memories of good things. I would be so deeply asleep that I felt wide awake and I would have no idea that what I was feeling was the opposite of being alive and living. Instead of being living and alive and dreaming. Which back then was a kind of hoping.

I felt warm and safe and happy and loved and best of all I was not thinking. And then something happened, a noise from above me in the ceiling, or a pain in my ribs and side and my dream would become really bright which to me meant I was waking up, and while this was not the same as before I knew it was better than being awake and I would fight to sleep, I would fight not to wake up and my heart would start to race. This meant that back then always and by this I mean every time I would wake up with my heart racing and I would be covered with just the most horrible feeling. There had never been any exceptions.

No one memory entered my mind, it was just that as I became more aware of where I was not and my heart would race more or faster and I would feel, more than anything, hopelessness, and that really heavy feeling that is despair, that feeling that I was failing and that I was losing and this feeling was more like an emotion after a while and after realizing I could not wait even a moment longer I would leap up and lean over the sink and vomit, bile gross-tasting and hurting my chest and nose and whatever pathetic puke there was inside me dripping from my mouth to make strings of my hair. I did not cry but tears filled my eyes.

And then one day I stopped dreaming. Well, I stopped remembering my dreams, anyways. One day I woke up and it was, simply enough, morning. It was crazy. I did not feel at peace, because that was of course impossible, peace meaning that you are not at war, but I did feel calm. There was within me the feeling that I was complete, that I was alive and I was happy to be alive. The blanket against my skin felt smooth and I concentrated on feeling the blanket and on feeling my skin. What was usually sore, or what might have been hurting, was not. It did not. By which I mean hurt. I felt my breasts and experienced surprise. I caressed them with my hands.

My one psychiatrist, I do tell her some things, by which I mean I text her a lot more of what I think, or am thinking, even without her asking questions, because one, I am actually curious and two, because one hour is a long time to sit in silence. Even for me. My psychiatrist pushes me on this moment. By which I mean she wants me to say more. And Episode Seven even stupidly suggests that I jerk off. So dumb. I will tell you what I tell her, only because it is the only time I have made any of these people blush. Oh, people's faces get red around me all the time. But that is because they are embarrassed for this crazy situation we are all in whenever we are together. But this reaction was because of something I said on purpose and as a joke. And that was this.

I did not want to come. I wanted to go.

Ha. Funny stuff.

So this, me waking up not at war and thinking about my skin, this was going on for who knows how long. They get this right on the show. I had no interest in keeping track of my days. I never understood why a person would want to keep track of how long they were captured. It is not like making a mark would take up time. It is not like realizing how long you have been gone from everything that you know and love would be wonderful or fun to consider. And it is not like my mom and dad would not be able to tell me how many days, even hours right down to the minutes and seconds, I had been gone. Was missing.

One morning I opened my eyes and sunlight from my window hit the wall opposite my mattress, the light making this strange sort of shape because the cement was all weird and bumpy. And within this sort of rectangle of light which seemed to sort of bend, to follow the curve that was the wall, brighter than the sunlight was a woman. And it was Mary. And I knew it then and I know it now and as I watched I could hear behind me rain falling against the window and the sound of the wind as it would rise and fall and as the sky darkened Mary became brighter, a bright sort of scarlet flame and surrounding her was one of those what I now know are called aureoles silver and yellow and green and purple and it was pulsing. And she was crying. Not hard or anything, but tears fell from her eyes and when they did the concrete on the ground sighed.

Mary raised a hand and she told me how it was possible for me to escape from my chains. She explained how, after it rained, I could make myself slip and fall and how I would sprain first one ankle and then after getting up twist the other. She said that I must endure this pain and dry the rain and make my ankles worse. She told me to, once I was inside, beg Him not to chain my ankles. She explained how my plea would make His rage move and how this would make Him chain the choke chains tighter and she said that I should complain and complain to make Him even angrier so that He would chain my chains even tighter. This, Mary said, would make my ankles get all swollen. She raised her other hand and curled her index finger and said, This is important.

She spoke without speaking, her words like the wings of butterflies tickling my feelings. She explained how this would explain to Him my moodiness and how the swelling, how the swelling would like a fantastic idea rise and that the swelling would save me and she said that pain is temporary, something to be endured, and that it is because of pain that we are able to find our way home.

*Dry The Rain* gets at none of this. This is because they, which is to say the producers and the writers, well they know, like I have already said, that you do not want to believe in, or be bored by, or with, God. Or that God, by which of course I mean Mary as well, is capable of doing so much good. I wanted nothing to do with *Dry The Rain*, and I said as much. Only someone, I will not say who, I will only write that this someone was a someone we loved and trusted, a someone who was part of what you would call our circle, which was smaller than His cellar, a someone who had what everyone finally agreed was, for real, proof, by which I mean that someone close to me, a someone who was not in what you would call our circle, which could only mean my psychiatrist, not the one I had now but one of the many different ones I had in the beginning, well this one person or these people had told someone everything, which means she, or a few shes, I only was sent women to speak to, had made up everything because I literally had told her and everyone nothing that had not been posted or in some other way written.

Anyways.

This someone we loved had contacted my parents and told them that my story, in some way, was going to be told, my story was in pre-production as we spoke, and that I might as well go along and talk. Which of course meant I should go and get paid because this was happening, by which I mean what would become *Dry The Rain* did not have to have anything to do with me. We might own things, but we do not own what happens to us. Let alone our stories. By which I mean how one lives is then seen and told by other people. Because my mom was an already celebrity she knew how to get me the perfect agent and lawyer for entertainment.

My mom, who was still an anchor person and my dad, who still believed in God, called their lawyer too and everyone decided that there was nothing we could do. Of course they asked me after giving me all of the information and all of the time I wanted but I did not need any. I just shrugged and nodded because it was not like I could think of anything else to do. And because of that I sure did not have anything to say. I did not want my dad to have to work anymore if he did not want to. My mom, with or without the millions of dollars, would do what she was going to do and that is why I am writing this story, which is for her, because she has plans for my story, to tell what actually really happened as best as she is able. She does not always want to be an anchor person and would rather have her own show and make it something that is real and good and honest and true.

. . .

There is not too much to say after I agreed to talk. Like the song goes there were interviews, interviews, interviews, interviews. Something like at least four or more ninety-minute interviews just by themselves, me meeting with just the producers and *Dry The Rain's* head writers, I mean. My mom and dad were not happy about this, but I did not want my mom and dad around. By this I mean I asked them to stay away. I promised myself that if I did not know the answer to a question I would simply say I do not know the answer to that question. And I had no interest in lying, in making stuff up to mess with them. I would tell them what they wanted to know when I could and this was stuff that my parents and that no parents should be allowed to hear. And by this I mean even that stuff and those things I did not say.

Aside from this number of secrets I will forever keep, I told the producers and the writers just about everything. I understood what they wanted. I understood from other TV shows and what I had read about what other people had watched and were watching what people wanted to see. What they wanted to believe and more importantly what it was they could point out and say they did not believe. The producers, mainly, but sometimes certain writers would ask questions and I would text my answers. Once they understood they were not talking with a dummy they began asking harder questions, or at least talking about questions they had for one another in front of me like, The idea of an idiosyncratic use of language is really interesting for a character in this situation.

In her, someone said. Of course by which they, which happened to be a she, had meant my.

Yes, He would say, the word sounding like this one long breath. Of course. In her situation. So sorry. And then to me, But, um, do you say.

Some of them were not even from here but were British, I

think. And not really because they had accents, but because they did not, really, by which I mean have accents this is to say, but more because of how they spoke, by which I mean arranged, by which I mean the order in which they said their words. It was all confusing.

Do you think you could take it a, say, well how about just a bit further, then? Like, love. You have me there. No doubt about that. But I think we can go further. Why, love. Why, and more importantly, how. How does language function for a character in ….

And then he was cut off.

Jerry! In her situation, some other woman who was always around smiling, stepped in and just started talking.

Right. Right. Of course. No harm meant, pet. In her, in your situation. Consistency is of utmost importance to anyone in captivity, right? So think about how your use of language reflects that. The way you speak, which is how you spoke to that terrible, terrible man, this says quite an awful lot, no?

You are exactly wrong though, I typed. I was a little kid. A little girl. I never knew when He was coming for me. It was not, and I thought of a comparison. It was not like going to church, I typed. After being there so long I did not know what days were. Those times when He choked me? I might have been knocked out for two minutes or two days. In the beginning there was not necessarily light. He messed with my mind in that way. I think it was for fun, but for a while He put on a recording that was nothing but the sound of a baby crying. And then there would be nothing. And then there would be the music of the baby crying again but only this time for not as long. But it felt much longer.

Listen to me, Jerry. This is how my psychiatrist, not the one I have now, but one of the first ones, this was how she put it. There was, specifically, no conformity in the application of something, let alone that which is necessary for the sake of logic, or accuracy. Remember? He did not speak.

I nodded and I wrote, This. What she just said.

And then I hit send.

And then I added, using caps to shout, After the first or second week he DID NOT speak. No words at all. Other than the basic commands. Which I already told you about. I have already told you about all of this. I do not mind for my mom and for my dad answering your same questions, and I am used to all this boredom which to be honest I do find interesting. But I really am telling you all of the truth. I am not going to make anything up. Ever. If you ask me something again and again and then I start to wonder about the answer I will say I do not know. I am only here talking now because of my mom and dad. For my mom and my dad. Well, some things are none of your business. But even that I will tell you. If I can't tell you something trust me you will be the first to know. But that man. He would not speak. I talked because I was expected to. If not I would get a lesson. For those he liked to use the pouring part of His oil can. Like I was the Tin Man and was in need of some oiling. That and especially when it was cold out he liked to use a toaster oven. So I really don't know what you want me to tell you. You can make stuff up just as good as I can and supposedly even better because you write for your jobs.

And then I fired off as many of the devil and any angry emojis I could find, even though I was not mad. Just because. And because they took everything I did so exactly and seriously they would sort of quiet down. And I found and still find all apps pretty much fun and fascinating. So it was pretty easy for me to shut them up. Even if it was just for a little bit at a time.

. . .

I always get so surprised and even amazed when I hear someone say something about boredom. Boredom really has to be this new invention, and by that I mean in no way does boredom have anything to do with me. It is just something lucky for you, that you have and get to enjoy. By which I mean that for most of the time people have been around on Earth they have been working, and that is to put it lightly, just to stay alive. There is nothing at all boring in that. And then maybe even boredom is only something that has enough time to take place in a few countries, if you know what I mean. And you should.


Like so many of you, though, they just did not believe me. By which I mean that I was never bored. They were positive, by which I mean totally convinced and certain, that boredom caused me to do these, whatever, wild and crazy things. Or, to be more precise, that He did all of these things to make sure that I could never be bored. That He was always around. That He was, in one way or another, antagonizing me. While they, like me, didn't understand why He had me dry the rain, they never said so. They all had and shared their theories. Or they would just get mad and go off in different directions, by which I mean rant.

Well, surely she doesn't just sit around, day after day, doing nothing. The bastard must have said something. All abusers use language against their captors. We know this as fact. Maybe she forgot?

She forgot.

Or blocked it out?

Repression?

I bet you she blocked it out.

How is that different from repression?

Well according to Freud.

Guys, this might be pointless.

It is, if you listen to Ronnie.

It is if you listen to me.

Me? Who's that again? Haven't heard the name.

For real?

What?

He was talking about himself, you clown.

Oh. Well, paint my blush with a brush.

Attack the idea, not the person.

What is this, the Internet?

Maybe she needs a different counselor?

Think?

Do you want us to get your counselor?

Or a different counselor?

Don't you mean psychiatrist?

Same thing.

Yeah, I always thought it strange, her never talking to a man. Might produce a different result. Wait. I thought all she ever did was speak with men?

Here we go.

A priest? Isn't her family, the dad, religious? Do we know a priest? She's gotta have a priest. How about a priest?

Better not be Unitarian or we've, like, got another woman on our hands.

Well, you never know. Those Bleeding Deacons—

Shut. The. Fuck. Up.

Guys. The kid. She's Roman Catholic. Have you been here for any of this?

Guys. You know who is here for all of us?

Hey, yeah, you're right, Laney. And then, one of them talking to me, Sorry about all of that. It's just how we creative types work.

Or do not work.

Hey-o.

To me, this guy who looked like no one I have ever seen, said, May I ask you? And then, How, for example, did this man, your captor, tell you to dry the rain? I know that you've been over this, but I'm not sure that we've been over this. Specifically. Those of us in the room. He told you to dry the rain. But specifically? Not sure I understand. Can we go over this again? Maybe we missed something. Given that, as you say, the man, your captor, didn't speak, we should take a closer look at what he did say.

You must have been so confused. Freaking maniac. This was that woman producer. She was pretty, nice, and kind.

Abusers twist the meaning of words, they subvert them, they use language to create doubt, control. This was a man producer.

Subvert?

What?

Isn't she a part of this conversation? She's a part of this conversation.

And?

Speak English to her, man.

You know how intelligent she is, right?

Yeah, of course, but I thought that was more sort of relative.

Guys. Come on. She. I repeat. She. Is. Sitting. Right. Here. Come off it, already.

Words give order, specificity, someone else said.

What they wanted from me I could not give them. They wanted what I knew they, the writers mostly, called acts of resistance. They wanted, given I am so smart, a was. They wanted for me to use words and for me to just use the words I did use differently. They wanted to hear more about the dictionary. What they wanted was for me to have used more words with Him, which was impossible, because I could not go back in time. What they also wanted was for me to use more words with them and this was also impossible because there were not any more of them. Words, that is to say. By which I mean for me to use.

Still.

They wanted this made clear and they again and then again made this clear. Obviously they of course had their writers and they had writers who then worked and wrote for those writers but from me they would take whatever they could get. I knew that they sometimes took what I said and wrote the opposite of that, liking that much better. Something I told them had the potential to make my story more real. In one way or another. Not that my story was not real, but the more real I made it was better. They could not use too much of what I said exactly because too much truth is not possible to believe and so they needed more words from me so as to be able to change them.


The producers, not so much. But they, being writers, were very fascinated and what I would consider obsessed with His dictionary. They thought I had control. They thought I could, as they always called it, talking as if I was not right there, code switch. They always thought that what I was doing was code switching. While I do, I have no idea what they are talking about.

What they could not understand was that me talking or being ghost silent I just totally and completely tuned Him out. I did not care about Him and that is what is really crazy because that one morning and even if it was for only one minute, although of course it had been longer than that, I had. Cared about Him of course. Enough to be interested. But enough about any of that.

.   .   .

I had no guesses about who He was. I knew why He had me so why should I care is that something that, if I had cared about them, I would have asked them. I mean it really is crazy. They, like you, felt that I would just sit around that cellar all by myself and think all about specifics. But I did not. There was not some routine. So, and I do not know how I could make them understand this, how there just and simply were no specific changes. Which of course meant there were no specifics. Like His cellar, my home, my time when He had me was all this big circle. It was no different than any other life, and by that I mean what has already been said which is, What would life be if not all sorts of things we do over and over again and again? Even more than that, I, like I already wrote, knew what would set Him off, or, more yes than less, what would not set Him off. So, what you all are watching on your TVs? Whatever episode you are on? What you are watching for the first or the fourth time? What you go on and on talking about? It is wrong. It is every bit and all of it wrong. There is no possible way for me to, even if I wanted to, give you even mostly part of the story. Me doing that would be like two teams trying to replay the same exact basketball game, me telling my story. It is just not possible. All I can give is the final score.


Mary, though. This is interesting and certainly something I do very much like to think about. When she was crying I started crying as well. And it felt good, crying. It was sort of like what I remembered laughing was like, though after He had stolen me and even before that morning when Mary just appeared there I had never considered laughing. Not in what it felt like and I did not wonder if I would ever laugh again. What I felt was totally real and accurate and the tears made my eyes like these watery windows to look through and everything I saw was strange and blurry and how I knew how and that this was being done for me. By which I mean Mary showing up and appearing. My vision was broken so my mind could be put back together really wildly yet totally exactly and I understood what crying was for and that I would never cry again, both there where He had me living and once I escaped.

I knew that this, by which I mean me not crying, would hurt those who love me and that once we were together again I would be expected to cry, that they would want me to cry maybe because they thought it was normal but mostly because they would think it was not normal if I did not, which is to say cry. I knew they would think that because I did not cry I was broken, that He had broken me and while that is not true, I was only badly hurt but I am not in any way ruined, He is not that big of a deal. What is true is that yes, this is what happened and like everything you want it to be one way when there is only the way.

When the clouds cleared or the sun broke through the clouds and the wind died down and the rain was swept away all got still and I fell asleep. I knew, as in I had known, that Mary was real, but it was really and truly wonderful to know even just a little bit more. With just a little more positivity. Now I know what you will say. How can I possibly know? I am lying. That was just hope, you, the nicer people out there, would say. Just like any really and truly religious person I can never prove it. By which I mean anything. And I cannot. By which I mean as in ever. But that would also mean that I would want to. Which is something I really do not care about. Proving anything, that is. But I just know that I have not had a dream since that time I met Mary, and I know that I never will again. Time passed. And maybe you can explain to everyone how it was that I managed to get away and escape. Because one thing you cannot say that I cannot say is, Here I am. Here where the world presents itself in simple geometry, by which I mean squares, mostly. By which I mean the tops of concrete buildings.

Someone I like wrote that the universe is in us. I agree.


The morning I killed Him I woke up and thought, This will be the day you kill Him. I did not think I would fail and I knew I would kill Him until He died and the only other thing I was worried about was getting really hurt, which might then pose a problem and was nothing that Mary had talked about.


Like I had felt my hair growing long for many what I considered weeks, I felt His footsteps overhead. Still, I was warm in my bed and it was still very dark. The way I slept is how I still sleep now and this was the fault of me in the beginning being both very scared and very cold, and when you are scared that of course makes you feel colder. There is no significance to this, despite how they, which is to say the producers and the writers, intentionally make it seem on *Dry The Rain*. I could not call into a ball, what you would call the fetal position, although that had been my instinct. There is a reason for this, and that was, and for a few different reasons, it just hurt too much. So yes, it is true, I did lie like I was in a coffin, but not exactly. Flat on my back with my hands rested like someone had placed them there softly, just so. What you would call in a state of repose. But this was, and is not so. My arms were crossed but tightly, with my hands in my armpits, and I would sleep like that, hugging myself warmly. Today, by which I mean tonight, I don't hold on so tight.

That it was dark meant it was still early, though not too early and so that meant we were going to get bad weather. Like a bird or some other animal I learned to understand when to be ready for rain. For snow. Pain like a line sort of built up in my ears to stretch across my forehead. The light from the humidifier glowed its bright green. The lights on the sensors glowed their bright red beneath my blankets. I did not want to hear His footsteps just yet, so I put my head under my blanket and this did quiet the sound somewhat and made it so that I was like in this small and quiet red room where you might develop photographs. I used this time to watch in my mind what I knew was about to happen. My breath made everything warmer.

As usual I had time as He stomped on down the steps. I was sitting on the end of the bed reading about the word simulation. By now as you might imagine I had read every word in that dictionary. Some more than others as well. The words I read the most I understood the least, if you know what I mean, although you probably do not. Which is fine. I understand. This is something that I just feel no one tries to understand. Not that point about the words, but about what people call coincidences.

What people do not understand is that I cannot point to my life and say, That right there is one coincidence. Because once He took me all that I had left was choice. Sure, if He was going to sodomize me He was going to sodomize me. But not to be gross, it was my choice if He was going to have an easy time or even if He was going to end up, assuming that He wanted to, having His way with a corpse. In another way of wording this, how I acted meant what was going to next happen and I know you do not believe me and that, if you just stop and think about this, that is your choice. By which I mean you could try and believe me for once. At least about something like this.

. . .

While not exactly so, simulation is what I think of as one of those words that people mix up and confuse with luck. Which a dictionary would tell you means a time when a person has something good happen or something bad happen brought upon by chance.

But then that should have you thinking, Well, what is chance? Aside from chance being that it is possible for something to happen, this means basically, again according to something like a dictionary, which is something that people agree with or really count on or turn to for something to agree upon, chance is something that happens without there being any real obvious sort of pattern or design.

But then that should have you thinking, Well, what about fortune? Which a dictionary would tell you is like chance or luck being this outside or random force. Which is not how He got me. Me getting taken and stolen had nothing to do with luck or chance because of course they do not exist. Those are just words. Concepts.

So like luck and fortune and chance, simulation is a word I do not think a lot of people really understand. Which I do not either and so I find it interesting and I have an understanding not because of its definition, but because of the words used in its definition. So the fact that I read books about simulation, which is one of the things that people who study me and not for *Dry The Rain* think is interesting, is because just as when compared to other words, as opposed to worlds or something, I find the definition really interesting. The reason for this being should be, and not if you just ask me, kind of obvious.

But to take from something I have read, when you lose someone, like my mom and dad did, it is easy to see patterns that are not there. Like you might see on the Internet and inside virtual reality and on TV. The things being important are not those that are made, by which I mean those things you can buy and hold, but that which you can turn on and see. Like how there is no way of even speaking about one thing and have another person get what you are meaning because everything depends on what you have heard and seen. And how that has been put together and produced by whomever. There are still things of course but what is most important is not what you get but what you put out for others to receive and it is more important to create content than to make babies is one way this might be said. That, and that everyone you meet is a producer or a writer. If you were looking for another.


When I was ready to kill Him until He died I did not often see Him, but when I did and especially lately it was like even though this certainly could not be so, He wanted to give me notice, a bit of privacy, now that I was older. Sort of like my father does for me now before coming into my bedroom to ask me a question.

By then I did feel edgy. This is because I was ready. For the past week like Mary had instructed I had been sullen. You might disagree, but this is not as easy as it might seem. Anything I had to be angry about I had forgotten long ago. I lived to exist. But more than this I was in pain. And it was hard to hurt and to act irritated at the same time. My ankles and the tops of my feet were fat and swollen and they were purple and green like storm clouds and pain. The pain was this heavy solid thing, like my chain. It felt like part of the chain, moving from the cellar floor in this line, like a bloody pulsing vein, to my hip. It was a definite misery that I understood as something that had to happen and part of something really good, something that would not last forever. I know this is a point of controversy. Me spraining my ankles. How, or even if, such a thing is possible. Well, it is. And, if only for your, to use a big word, edification, here is the how.

The main thing I'll say, by which I mean the idea I want to write that is the most important to me, is that it takes way more bravery than you think you have inside you. Even after you have how forever long been with a man like Him, by which I mean months but especially something like years, you realize that bravery and courage are just these very different things and you, by which I mean me, come to see that this is because He found activities like spraining or simply bruising things as interesting as most kids see going to church. Why sprain someone's ankle when you can put someone's hand in a pot of water and turn up the heat and while it boiled wait to see how long it took before a girl, her wrist locked in place, louder than any lobster, started to scream? Or how long it would take a girl before she would actually become willing to hurt and injure a puppy or a kitten? So I was surprised by how hard it was for me to actually do what Mary had said, which wasn't really that complicated.

What Mary told me to do was this: Jump.

She told me to jump, and then, while landing on the side of my foot, as opposed to how you would like a normal person, really and truly let all my weight, as in from the top of my head and down through my knees, push into the ground. Obviously this is something I needed to do when He was not at home. Also obviously if I was outside I would be there for the purpose of drying the rain, which of course meant the ground would be wet, and Mary told me to look for the wettest, by which she meant slipperiest spot possible, because this would cause me to actually, as in naturally, by which I mean as naturally as something like this can be, slip. What I won't do is tell you how many times I tried to jump and then, as opposed to how you would like a normal person, land on my foot's side, all the while thinking to push down from the top of my head through my knee without, and this is an important part I forgot to mention, falling, landed normally. I won't mention exactly how many times I just wasn't brave enough. But I will tell you about the time I was able to do so, and you'll just have to believe me that doing it again, by which I mean a second time, on my other foot, knowing all the puke-making pain that was coming, was way more than two times more difficult.

While more yes than less His yard was perfectly flat, as if He had at some point dug up the area and then steamrolled, or whatevered it flat, which, as you all know from watching *Dry The Rain* episode one, early on, that part where they show the FBI and the police digging up His backyard and finding however many different parts of bodies, by which I mean, except for two, nothing but what you would call skeletal remains, He did, and so there were parts of His backyard that weren't as flat, and you, by which I mean me, would find some small bumps that created little indents, or indents that created little bumps, however you want to look at it. And while there were never any what I considered puddles, you, by which I mean me, would find a few spots that took much longer to dry than others. Of course I knew where all of them were, and I went to the tallest bump, or the deepest what I guess is best called depression, and, after standing on one foot, sort of like a flamingo, jumped.

.  .  .

Before this, to calm my body and mind into thinking I wasn't about to do anything that every part of my mind and body told me was going to hurt, I stood, not yet like a flamingo, staring at my bird, the cute blue chubby one, who was sitting, by which I mean standing, on top of the fence. He never really said too much, but my favorite thing was that when he did speak, by which I of course mean chirp, what he said sounded like a question. I now know there are better ways to spell this, but back then it sounded like Two are we? which, of course, I thought was the best thing, one, because it gave me a chance to speak, which, to be more precise, I mean respond, by which I mean to think my answer. The second reason I loved listening to him speak was because I didn't really understand the question. On one hand, I knew that him being one, and me being one, that made two, but his question made me wonder, We are two? Or, on this other hand, I thought, maybe he meant we are too. As in too much. As in us, being we, is too much to be.

And so I was thinking about this, and feeling the sun, and the wind was blowing my hair when I decided that then was as good a time as any to, at least, stand like a flamingo. I told myself that I would jump when he flew away. And that if he didn't fly away, and I got too tired, I would try spraining my ankle another day. I left the decision to God. To Mary. In this way I wasn't really thinking, or I was thinking so much without realizing it, as if my bird had given me what I now know is a koan, and this particular koan, those words that my bird had given me, is a gift, by which I mean a present I can never repay and of course for whatever reason, which wasn't, in case you are wondering, to help me by the way, he just flew away for one of the great many reasons birds fly off, all of which has nothing to do with me and all of which is to say is that my mind was pretty blank when he flew away and I jumped and I landed on the side of my foot exactly perfectly and with my mouth open and a scream screaming in my mind I let all of my weight fall through me.

I was not able to stand. The pain was like this bright twinkling agate lightning shiver that I saw sparkling behind my closed eyes and I puked, the pink strawberry shake I had for lunch I sprayed with very great surprise off to the side and because the shake was thick some of that pink strawberry goo got caught in my throat, which got me to coughing, by which I mean the stuff really felt stuck and thick as cement and I because I thought I was having trouble breathing I focused on that, forgetting for a moment about my foot, and when I stood up the pain was so sharp, by which I mean it was like I was stung by a bee as big as a beaver, I fell back down and without thinking I did what Mary said which was grab my foot and bend it inwards and hold it until I couldn't, and then bend it the other way until the pain got too great and I couldn't, and if Mary or God was looking down at me while I know they were happy, which is to say pleased, I wonder how much pity they took. By which I mean if any.

And yes the pain before it got better was much worse. It was a definite misery that I understood as something that had to happen and part of something really good, something that would not last forever. I could do this.

This would be it.

I knew this because the other day, by which I mean not long after He saw I had hurt myself, me indicating to Him that I slipped, that I tripped when drying the rain with my foot, which was something easy enough for Him to believe because He, of course, had seen me using my putter foot to dry the rain, well that one day when He tied up my other ankle tighter than even usual I did not scream and even though Mary told me to I could not, by which I mean say anything, but I did what I knew was the next best thing, which was itself like both writing and screaming. I spit.

And yes, of course. I injured, by which I sprained my other ankle. I hurt my other foot. But you will never believe just, exactly, how. So watch *Dry The Rain*. Maybe you will see.


From this part on you know what happened, mainly. By which I mean when I killed Him. And, really, I do not blame you for doubting. Who am I to say how I would be were you me and I were you? Even though you have not seen the episode people have and so you have heard and you also know what happened because what happened was written about and posted all over the Internet. This part of my ordeal was made more of a bigger deal than a little kid my age being sodomized, rape being not really that big of a deal and sort of expected to happen to girls taken and stolen like me. Or not even when taken and stolen, to be totally exact. People would and still do comment on my size. That I was tiny but tall. How I am a girl but strong. What happened is this.

I watch His scissors in His back pocket as He stomps up and then down the steps. Up and then down the steps. You know, the usual. I do not think He means to stomp, He is just really heavy, by which I mean what you would call big-boned. I never really thought this but knowing this I can see Him as the sort of guy working on cars. Not that I was thinking about this, then. I grab my dress and pull it over my head. This is where they get that famous scene from and picture that they use for the Blu-ray case of the *Dry The Rain* series that you will eventually be able to buy, that wild image of me, by which I mean Mallory, barefoot staggering early in the morning down the middle of a gray and foggy and tree-lined street. Of course I am not naked. I am as I was in my white dress, only back then my dress was not white, it was not tastefully spattered in blood but rather mostly black and crimson from having soaked up so much of His blood, and, I suppose, dirt. I deeply breathe as He sets the mirror before me. In its way the pain is comfortable because it is calming and gives me something to think about. I am like a drawing colored in with markers. I feel stronger. He hands me the scissors. The same pair after all of this time together. It is kind of too bad I did not take them with me.

Staring at the scissors He wants me to cut my hair, He wants me looking a certain way. I know I am about to kill Him but I think, Still. Still, He still wants me to cut my hair. He wants me to look a certain way. Me cutting my hair and looking a certain way will make that more fun and more pleasant what-ever He later has planned for me. I stare at the cat's feet. After thinking without thinking I grab and make as much of a fist of my hair as possible acting just like the scissors is a saw. I saw more than I cut through my hair and I do this with such violence that I cut my scalp. I do not poke a hole or anything or slice up this deep gash but I would say I make a pretty big cut because my hand and then my ear are warm with thick blood.

Good.

More pain. And blood.

I throw the hair at Him and it lands on the floor in its clump and I shove the scissors in the mattress and howl and I have not heard my voice outside my head in so long that I feel the mad rush of understanding. It feels like smiling. When He comes rushing His face, a face, His, which for as long as I can remember has been twisted-looking and crooked and sort of pulled back as if caught by something, well now this was a face, His, His was a face that, suddenly, and totally, had straightened, He looked, if you didn't look at His eyes, calm, maybe almost happy, and with His one fist raised to punch my face I get lucky. When I yank the scissors from the mattress and with pain screaming in my feet I jump up and leap and I stab Him not in the cheek, which is where I was aiming, but in the eye. With my hand still gripping the scissors He sort of falls to His knees, but more onto His hip. Blood warm as blood splashes my face. My chest.

Before this sensation there was for a moment this feeling which was like I was stabbing air and I could feel so much of my arm and my elbow, like I was working really hard to throw a pinecone. If you know what I mean. Which, by now, most of you do. My pinecone game being this online game, if not challenge, that you, for a different sort of fun, spend time filming. And then posting. Anyways. It was that sort of feeling. At the end of my arm there being nothing real and so I felt the other parts of my arm all that much more and so that hurt as well.

At first He does not scream and so I hear the squish. This squoosh. More made by my mind, an invention, I am sure, this sound. Because who has ever seen anything like this before. Not even on TV or even the Internet I am sure. But how sweet and pretty. If I was made to make music, this was the music I was made to make. And then I felt a blast of pain as bright as metal.

My wrist jammed when I struck the back of His skull. I was holding the scissors like you imagine, with my hand wrapped up there near the handle and I was stabbing of course downward and so it was like I had stabbed His rock wall. The pain was direct.

Still thinking but without really thinking I pulled the scissors from His eyeball and blood slipped from His open mouth and I began stabbing Him more like in the neck. Or that really soft area between His neck and His shoulder, right where there was all sorts of room. In and out in and out. All of this blood that was really red and warmer than what came from me squirted on and across my face, my open eyes. Repeatedly. Again and again. Over and over. More. Of me. Stabbing Him.

He kept on reaching for me. He raised His other hand to His eye and I stabbed Him and stabbed Him again and there was more blood but like anything with more holes in it He was leaking faster and I was breathing now really hard like I had been running and I kept at it and I kept at it after I watched Him stop moving and then stop breathing and then kept on as I watched Him doing nothing. There are many ways for us to die and back then I was not sure of any of them. So it was not long before I moved on to the chain.


I know this now for a fact, but I knew that there was no reason for Him chaining me other than like I said He was really smart and took extra care. And so if He taught me anything it was that I was not a doctor and so I was not going to leave something like Him being even just a little bit alive a possibility.

My feet yes they did hurt and even more so if I thought about them so of course I did not think about them and just considered my chain, the one that I was basically always wearing. I sort of slid and I guess you could say scooted off my mattress until I was close enough to His face to have all of this total access. I considered what there was I could do and in what order. I was not psycho, but I for sure was not what you would call squeamish.

His one eye had definitely what I call popped like one of those rubber eyes you see during Halloween, and like a popped water balloon most of what I considered the left-overs, by which you can picture rubber, was there, it was together, but there were other pieces of this on His eyebrow and down by His lip. I picked them up. Sort of like what I think it would be like to pick up a dead jellyfish the bits seemed to slide and squirm and they seemed to sort of shrink and shrivel in my fingers. I wiped my hands on His hair.

With two hands I picked up a part of the chain and strong as I was I did grunt when I lifted it up and I do think I screamed because of the pain in my feet but especially the one, the first one I sprained, the left, the club that I used to dry the rain, and then I did almost sort of drop it when I brought it down on His face. I think this was my subconscious thinking because the side of one link smashed that big fat Santa nose of His and His face just sort of exploded. There really was not much to see because the skin that was all over His nose covered everything.


Of course they show all sorts of crazy violence during *Dry The Rain*, but they do not explain any of it, as in the whys as opposed to the ways. The FBI guys had all sorts of questions about what happened and how, but all I did was shrug. But because I know some of you genuinely care I will share this. I did get sort of curious. Nothing more. Nothing less. I mean of course I knew He was dead. But this, by which I mean the last thing I did, was not overkill. That is a promise.

.   .   .

The last thing I did was take a chain and use it like a rope. I grabbed with one hand a clump of His hair and I lifted His head. I dropped His head. I made an X with the chain across His neck and for a minute I considered undoing His boots and using His laces to strangle Him as well but I did not have any interest in seeing His socks or His feet and so while it was not as easy I strangled Him with His chains and the weight of that metal or steel or whatever it was made up for the fact that I could not really tie them or make a knot and He definitely must have had plenty of air and oxygen inside Him, I guess all those holes did not matter all that much because His face turned bright red as a butterfly. This, which is to say His face, became a sort of blue. But that might have been what you call the power of suggestion because do not forget everything I am telling you is coming from my memory.

I remembered one thing Mary told me. Well, to be exactly precise, I suppose I never forgot. Even though I did not want to at all I moved my really sore and swollen foot to the side and I closed my eyes and I lifted the other chain as high overhead as I could and then before giving myself a second to think I threw the chain on my foot as hard as I could and I puked and kind of fainted but I was done.

It took days for the swelling to subside. My feet and ankles. For the pain that existed in my ankles and feet there is no word. At least not that I know of. So I am unable to properly express its nature. Its form. This is because pain exists outside of category, even though we pretend differently. But this was not pain on a scale from one through ten. My pain was not some red, ready-to-pop un-smiling face emoji. So in this way, by which I mean absent metaphor and exciting diction, my pain becomes possible to describe. Just like, if you care to pay attention, the rest of me.

In time I felt much better. A day or two after that point in time I realized much of that, by which I mean feeling better, had to do with all of the excitement, by which you might say adrenalin, associated from when I jumped up to kill Him and then kept on killing Him until He died. And then of course what I did when I was done. But I did not know how much time had passed because I did not keep track for I was not in this big hurry. I was not bored or anything. If I had been like an octopus and how they, by which I mean when one is in captivity it will eat its own arms, I would have done that a long time ago. I would have had no hands to kill Him. Or time on my hands to kill, as far as that goes.

And so it was not one of those sorts of things. It was either boredom or me. Only one of us could be. And even though I knew He was dead I did enjoy and had fun thinking He was still a little bit alive and that I was watching Him die and that He might get up and attack me and so in self-defense I needed to stab Him now and then. Part of this was not because I was demented, because yes, it was pretty horrible. It is not that I liked having His body there. As my ankles got less swollen He got puffier and our bodies became a kind of a minute and second hand. It was almost time. And yes. This is the sort of information the FBI found interesting.


More than anything I was not quite ready to see anybody, and if He did not start smelling so bad I am pretty sure that I would have stayed longer. If I had the sound of my humidifier running I would have stayed longer. If I had food and did not get so hungry I would have stayed longer. If it had been warmer I would have stayed longer. If.

Do not get me wrong. I loved my parents, but what I felt was weird, the sort of love I felt when, during what I figured to be the week, He left the house and I had running over me and through me the warmth of knowing I was alone. I knew that this feeling would change but I also knew that in leaving I was about to enter a whole new world of weird. Being in His cellar was like being in a desert. It was real alright. It was so real that everything was basically made so small that what I lived through were just these couple of things you could always see around you and it did not matter what direction you turned to. They would just be there. When I left things were going to get way real and so fast and so big I just knew it would just be so much. And I was right.

When I did get home everyone thought I was broken and wanted to help if not fix me then to help fix themselves from feeling so strange and weird about everything. Of course everyone felt badly for me and even worse they felt bad for feeling bad for themselves because they never expected to see me again and had long ago known I was dead. Only here I was. I was in their living rooms. Or I was on the TVs in their living rooms, which was way different from what they expected to be watching, and of course even worse than TV because and here I am not talking about *Dry The Rain* but the news, I was all over the Internet which I fast saw most people wanted, if they had to watch it at all, made funny. They felt, I knew, because my mom explained how even people we knew and were in our lives and were acting towards me, they felt this strange sort of guilt combined with this worry that I could never forgive them for knowing I was dead and not only did they just go on living but because, like my mom put it, they had moved on with living. Which is to say they felt bad about having been happy while He had me and they just knew I was dead. But it's cool, though. I get it.

My mom and my dad were pretty cool or at least they acted so and I really wanted to ask my mom about Uncle Billy but when it came to me feeling anything the only thing I felt was worry. A worrying feeling I could not name.

I had always loved my uncle and we had always been close so I knew something was wrong because two weeks after I left the hospital I still had not heard from him. And I did not exactly get reunited with my mom and dad and sent to Endwell General directly, so a decent amount of time had come and gone and I had not even heard his name. And believe me this was strange. As much as I loved my uncle I knew that he loved me just as well. So Why and Where is he was something that I wondered. And by that I mean I wondered much more about the Why, which is something I will soon get to.

Because everything was possible, including him being dead, or worse, I did not want to go asking my mom and dad about the where. This was because if the answer was sad because at that time I did not know if two people together could be happy and after having been the reason for them feeling so terribly and for so long I did not want to go on doing or saying anything to mess that up. And so I did wait. And I am not sure if I ever did ask or if I just more yes than less found out for myself.

I know that he was scared. And obviously I do understand. I was no longer his kid niece.

I had turned into this young woman, or, I guess back then it is better to say I was turning into this young woman, who had been, he knew, thanks to the Internet, brutalized with a turkey baster, my juices collected for cat food, I guess He had two cats, and salad dressings. And then one day he called.

He had moved to Massachusetts because my aunt got this great job with Lego but he had driven to Endwell and he was staying at the Relax Inn which was basically in walking distance. None of this had been planned. I guess he was just ready and got in his car and drove. He called our home and he spoke with my mom and they talked for a while and although she gave me the phone I did not want to take it from her because it was so nice to hear her laughing which was something she was slow to do. Plus, what was I going to say? My mom forgot that sometimes. And other times she had ways of trying to get, by which I mean trick me into speaking. If I was up for it, he said, he wanted to take me sailing.

Tomorrow, he said.

And then, No pressure.

I smiled listening to the sound of his voice.

Not talking was easy. I nodded.

My mom took the phone and then spoke for me. He knew that I was only listening, so she told him that I said Yes and that I looked excited, which I am sure I did.

I loved and still love the water and I really loved sailing. Which I may have said. Like everything, nobody had asked me to do anything that I loved doing before He took and stole me. I am not sure I know the reason for this. People thought they remembered more about me than I did, given how little I had been. I do know that much. But I also know that people were just all shook up and thought of me like a ghost. I mean for sure. I get it. For basically everyone I did come back from the dead. And for probably my uncle, too. But what made him different was that, however this was possible, he understood. He had always understood. That what happened to me wasn't about him, or my mom or my dad, or anyone. What he understood always was that I had a life to live, like anyone, and that because usually anyone, when noticing someone they loved was going through something tough, like to make their lives easier by making their loved one feel okay and, in that process, no longer a burden. For Uncle Billy life didn't work like that. Your pet cat was alive until it wasn't. That the pet cat was yours, not his, was the difference. He gave you space to process grief. Regarding Him? Uncle Billy knew there was never going to be anything to do or to say. But he loved me. He knew I loved him. And so he waited. He gave everything time. Until not the right, because there would never be a right, he just waited until one day.

My mom hung up the phone. She offered to give me a ride but I told her, by which I mean I wrote, No thanks and, It was okay and, I did not think so and, That it would be nice to take my bike.

Waking early, I did not eat breakfast. This was one thing that worried a lot of people, how little I was eating. But I was never hungry. I never really got over how much of eating was drinking, and I knew I would never drink even a Shamrock Shake ever again. That morning my mom was making bacon and this is true, like you do read in a lot of books, smelling stuff, especially food, and for me especially breakfast meats, raised memories just as deep purple as a bad bruise. And eating when you are not hungry and thinking about Him is not easy and in my opinion way over the top for people to ask of you and just about one of the worst things to do. Also, although I never got into this before, I ate, because if I did not eat there would be an issue with Him. A lesson. And He loved teaching. So I knew that forever food and eating was going to be an issue. I did drink some apple juice, though. I did eat most of a piece of toast. And then I rode my bike to the Relax Inn and I walked a flight of steps to his room and I held my breath and waited and I watched what was going to happen.

The door is open and Uncle Billy sits on the end of the made bed staring at the turned-off TV. I can see his shadow reflected on the screen and he does not try to speak. I watch him try to lift his drink but even on the glass screen I can see this is not easy and I step over and stop my feet right before him and I put my hand on his shoulder. I take his coffee and set it on the end table. And I give the first hug I have given anyone since I killed Him. Of course my mom has hugged me and my dad has hugged me but that was at first and they do not try to touch me so much now. My hair which had to be cut short so it does not look ridiculous is still a bit long and this falls across his back and I can feel his tears on my shoulder, they are so warm and wet and I see His stone floor cellar and it is not easy for me to swallow and I stand like that for some time with him sitting and even though I can smell the ocean my mind is not thinking.

He looks the same and I of course am different but what existed between us fills the room, this has not changed and finally I do not feel like a gray ribbon, a sign stapled to a telephone pole. He does not say much as, more quietly than silently, I watch him gather a few things and I see how he moves with purpose, how it is that he hasn't really planned things, that his mind has really been on me, and after he packs his cooler with some food and some drinks from the hotel's tiny fridge we make for his truck.

Later I will have a sunburn and I will have windburn but my mom will only smile when I come inside smelling of the sea and sand and by now she knows better than to ask questions but I sit at the kitchen table and I cannot tell her about my day or anything about my time in the cellar which is what I know she wants and she cries and I cannot blame her, I am her daughter, and while I do not hug her I will reach across the table and touch her arm. Her hand.

The morning is perfect. From a little wooden bridge, a boy and his mom feed a family of ducks. Seagulls are fixed, tethered points in the sky, their cries carried away with the high, racing wind. There is nothing to envy and there is nothing to despise. We park and walk across a perfectly manicured lawn. It is a Saturday morning and the world is still.

We make for a slip on Ketchum Creek. A log breaks the water's surface. That place where, in the middle of the morning, turtles bask in sunlight. A frog either sunk in or pushing through green-black algae as green and black as the frog itself. Sunlight makes pinpricks of its eyes. Against the wooden wall is a pretty heron and it is sleek and it is graceful and I cannot say if it is asleep or if it is awake. Dragonflies dip and skim across the water. Hovering, rising and falling, suspended in air. Impossible movements. And in these creatures and in their movements no great mystery greater than any other. This is because while people are created to be amazed they are not prepared for what they encounter. At least not really.


My uncle, who does not sail much, has friends who do, and he borrowed *Leigh Fordham* for the day. At twenty feet the boat is much bigger than I expected. Uncle Billy says the cool thing about this boat is that you can leave the backstay and side shrouds attached. Everything is in its right place, except for the forestay, but there is a remote control in the cabin. This makes rigging easy.

It is magic.

We push off.


Ketchum Creek is narrow but becalmed and so are we and after heading up a bit we ease into attitudes cool as the water. Cattails rise near docks. A slow trickle of water feeds from some pond I cannot see. Here the water runs black and clear, and water lilies sway on the water like bright green objects carefully arranged. Blue water lily flowers with their long pedicels glow bright as lit candles. The boat seems reliable and I look forward to the open sea, lowering the rail a bit, sitting up on the coaming. There are beautiful homes on either side of the creek. Mansions, really. What safety. What security. I look through open windows and little children wave and I smile, I raise my hand.

Here, where nothing bad can happen.

Home, where there is a certain sort of protection.

. . .

Soon, we sail through an inlet. And then the world itself. At first just shapes in the distance, a feeling of place not so much boundless as free of borders, definitions. Greater dunes now rising wild as ancient limestone hills, access roads, meaningless turn-offs, plateaus treeless, all of it threatening and all of it living. Way out on some faraway shore a string of small shacks, echoes of color. Life would be fairer were our days defined as asleep and awake. As beautiful. And then before us like a mirage of a bridge in the distance is a bridge in the distance and the Atlantic Ocean, too. Water so vast and so blue as to become something to doubt.

You okay?

I nod. Uncle Billy comes closer and checks my life jacket.

The clouds look like fists. Wind rising from the water erases all noise, an end to all but the whip of the self-erasing wind. There is a light chop, enough bluster disturbs the water's surface to create fierce, jagged points of light. Far away tall grasses flattening, shapeshifting, in sound a distinct rattle, like something almost unnatural. Marshes extend. In some other distance a lighthouse.

He shrugs, says, Be crazy if after all that psycho-killer bullshit you drown in some boating accident.

I smile.

Nothing to do now but just sail for a bit. Guess the stripers are out there, a ways. If even at all. I'm going to check out the cabin. Put our lunch in the fridge. Make a call if that's alright. Then I thought maybe we could fish. Well, at least that I could, anyways.

I nod.


Fish.

It is funny. There are very few sights, or smells, that, once seen, or smelled, bring Him to mind. People try to figure out why, but who knows. Still, though, there are words. Someone might say something, or I might hear the way something is said and thoughts of Him, like bubbles in bathwater, rise to the surface and pop. They burst.

As much as I do not like fishing and find so much of it to be cruel there is another part of me that sees in the sport this cosmic sort of power. It is hard to believe that a lure will attract a fish and that a fish will try to eat the lure and that there, resisting on the end of your line, is an animal, something so small in so huge a space as an ocean, an area of this, our world, that should not be contained by a name, because what are names if not words encircling our imaginations and you think that you, of all possible things, in so much incredible and impossible space, caught it. That you tricked the fish.

I look in many different directions and it is amazing, the waves, the water unfolding like creases upon a crumpled sheet of paper. I lean forward. What my uncle calls the offing approaches, as opposed to draining away, and how the sky seems to rise only to collapse in upon itself and we are no more closer to the water now and the endless approaching fold of the ocean's cresting waves than we were before and how all of this, so gentle and calm, yet wild and absent restraint, seems patterned, prearranged, and it is almost without thinking, it is almost with careful deliberation that I finish what I have been thinking.

Like a photograph dipped in solution and left to bloom I wait for a picture to emerge, checking out how the shapes bend and seem to breathe, how they rise from deep recesses to become lighter darknesses, patterns emerald green, deep and rich, receding to return these deep sea creatures of my mind, phosphorescent and bioluminescent in erratic bursts gelling, working to make of everything eerie underwater blue fissured with a network of lines stark like bolts of lightning. I feel different sounds. They arrive as distractions.

I had gone fishing since that first cast. The one I told you about. At the end of the dock. Rising from a lake that is better remembered. I never imagined or thought of the words capturing, swimming, pulling, terror, free.

What I did, though, was feel.

And whenever I hooked a fish I became a little more horrified, and then more than a little horrified until, finally, one final time, I turned, handed the rod to my dad, shaking and dizzy until the fish was caught and let free.

And then, like that, that was it for me.

I look over the side of the boat. The foamy water, a blue or a gray sort of white or green is like a mirror on fire and I see Him and I realize that my uncle left to give me some space, some time to think and this is why I love him and Crayola does not make a color to describe Him, although the ocean, or at least the Bay, whatever this is, I have not been here since I was a kid, comes close. Its colors, I mean.

In time His face, which was very white, turned a sort of purple and then this greenish-gray, just like an old black eye, and then that sort of gray you find on the bottom of old white socks. This is hard to believe and of course many of you will not, which is something I totally understand, but I really do not mind when something happens and I find myself thinking about Him. This is nothing I set out or want to do, but it does happen and I do not mind. How His wrinkles, like a wet paper towel, disintegrated. How He did become very stiff in that manner particular to rigor mortis. And then how He softened. How He got so soft. His good eye open. His other eye, having popped, no longer really being an eye, the stuff of what remained running down the side of His face, hardening like the white part of a cracked egg, by which I mean the albumen, on the side of a frying pan, or the top of a range. For some reason He died with His hands raised before Him and they stuck like that, frozen, suspended in air, so that He looked like a tiny T-Rex. Until they didn't. Until His hands fell to the floor. I did not smile, or laugh, but warmth spread throughout my body and I again considered what it meant to smile, to laugh, and as much as I wanted to smile, or laugh, like vomit I kept it down.

Strangely, His face melted. At least I think so. These memories being mine, me being the only one to have them, there is no one to say if I am right or otherwise when I get it wrong. It was as though whomever had been reeling Him in cut bait. The tip of His tongue—that tongue—lolled from the side of His mouth. I snipped it off with His scissors and a bit of blood oozed and squirted like when you squeeze a ketchup packet. And then I planted the scissors back inside His face.

For days I slept, as often as I could, with my feet raised high up on the sink. This did a couple of different things. First, the choke chains slid down towards my knees, however naturally. I would work them, hour after hour, up and down, up and down, the metal cool against my calves, hard against my knees, the tension releasing. Second, the swelling in my ankles stopped. It took a while. Maybe four days total, but, like I said, I was not counting. And I saw things in that cellar I did not want to see. Sometimes, I was not sure when I was awake and when I was sleeping. But finally, and with less pain than I imagined, I was able to sit up. I looked at my left foot. There was only a little swelling that I could see, and I was able to roll the stretched-out chain down my leg and over my ankle. The ankle on my club foot, I mean. In less time than you would think, this, by which I mean my chain, basically fell to the ground before I was even ready. This was because He had tied the chains to fit around my hurt and swollen feet. It was because I got one foot free, I know, that I was able to get through what I needed to, by which I mean in terms of patience and pain, and work loose the other chain.

It was weird. I wasn't chained.

Thanks, Mary.

It was not like I never walked and you all know I exercised but still I was stiff and my ankles were tender and I guess I was in a condition you could call shock. I knew I was going to kill Him. This I had known even before Mary visited. By which of course I mean before she talked to me about everything, which had nothing to do with how to kill Him, but how it was I was going to be able to get free. I was going to kill Him and I wanted to, I was really looking forward to it, but of course I did not know what it was going to feel like. That is another story. One that is only for me.

Anyways.

I took the scissors from His neck, I did not remember putting them there, and there was a puff of gas, sort of like smoke, and I dropped them in the sink.

I did not want to go up the stairs. I was not curious. For a moment I worried the door might have been locked. But He never locked the door when bringing down the mirror. There, in His mind, was no need. Upstairs, though. Every other possible door or window of escape was very locked. I always knew that it would have amused Him had I tried to escape and one thing I worked never to do was that. Amuse Him.

I walked to the wall and I placed my hand beside that place where Mary appeared. What had been Mary was, by which I mean literally, still as stone. This had to be. For a wall to be it could not be anything other than this. And the stone was cool and rough, by which I mean what I felt was what I expected to touch. But the stone was not still. There was a pattern swirling with these lines and streaks in these moving amounts of watery colors that were violet, indigo, blue, green, yellow, orange, and red. But, when not moving so much, mostly blue. Its shape, by this I mean the outline around, or maybe of Mary, was a little bit like a bottle and reminded me of a rainbow only it was like the rainbow was breathing and the stone was bumpy and had dimension and slight cracks otherwise invisible and a beautiful moonlike neon escaped the shape, like light from a lantern, and a beam shot to the ceiling, it flattened in a perfect circle above me and beside my hand the wall, like water streaming down a windshield, was crying. There is no other way for me to describe this. The humidifier hummed. I knew that I did not need forgiveness. That forgiveness was something I did not need. I walked outside.

The grass was soaking wet. The van and the patio furniture was soaking wet. The grill. My little and tiny tree. The sun had risen and later, much later, after the sun had completed its arc, after the sun had set below the hillside, color spread across the horizon. Like how gas catches fire and runs blue like a river across a bed of coals, these low-lying hillsides in outline. Electric blue. Deep purple and pink. And this color as night came on fading, the sky becoming like grains of that kinetic sand put in a bowl and shaken all about so I saw these different shades of orange and yellow and turquoise green sort of settling to become pretty before mixing to become blue and the black of moonlight night, distant stars bright and formless as scars.

It is okay.

I shrugged. I did what I had to do. I walked back into the cellar. I climbed the stairs. I found a phone. I found a bag of cellphones. I was not in a hurry. I looked through them and of course none of them had power. But of course it did not matter. Stranger Danger. I closed my eyes. And I dialed Nine and then One and then One.

Only it was the strangest thing.

Nothing happened.

Or at least that's how I remember it. That's how it seemed.

And so I dropped the phone. I went and I got His keys. I went to the front door. And I let myself free. Barefoot and bloody and tired and sore I started walking down some street.


Don't move, my uncle breathed.

I had not realized he was behind me. I did not move. But I saw what caught his attention. There was a bird, like a butterfly, flitting above my knee. Slowly, by which I mean I knew the feeling, the bird descended. It landed on my thigh. A blackpoll warbler it was and I studied it carefully and I hoped that it would sing.

.   .   .

The blackpoll, a songbird, weighs about as much as an empty soda can. I felt its little feet, that little bird clinging to my knee, as *Leigh Fordham* cut across the Bay. Every summer the birds appear in Canada and Alaska in hopes of breeding. They fly up the coast of North America from South America, going back year after year to the same spots along the United States' eastern seaboard to rest. This bird had lost its way.

The bird is pretty. Like me, the bird is unremarkable. Its crown is weathered and its feathers are disheveled, a mishmash of browns and grays, like it had been plucked by spoiled children. Tied to its back, like a sort of backpack, is a tiny, black, GPS tracker which lets people monitor the little bird. A little bird that, already, simply to survive, has too much to do.

But I was here, still as a pine tree, and so the bird figured why not. Flying, or migrating, this was not exactly some competition. And taking a chance was better than dying. Or, just like me, who knows what it is thinking.

I kept hoping it would sing, but no, it did not sing. My uncle might have spooked it. But maybe, by which I mean to say, No. Probably not.

The bird, rested, slowly lowering its weight onto my own, leapt like a spring.

And then it flew away.

People, human beings, are curious how blackpolls, as creatures, can pack up from a place like Nova Scotia and a few days later land on a tree branch in, say, Argentina. Some people suspect they do something remarkable, like fly across the Atlantic Ocean. This flight, lasting two or more days, would be quite an intense, incredible voyage for such a tiny, unremarkable bird.

A human, for example, would have to travel more than eleven million miles, without stopping, to do the same sort of thing.

So of course no one thinks this is possible.

But they do.

# ACKNOWLEDGMENTS

Richard Leise would like to thank the following people for their efforts in making this novel possible: John Duffy, Neil Griffiths, Joshua Trent Brown, John McManus, Luisa Igloria, Janet Peery, Kent Wascom, Manuela Mourao, Rebecca Bengal, my parents, my other parents: Ricky and Catherine, Jim H., Dan, Phinneas, Charlie, Julian, Zinnia, The STARS, Solomon, Toto, Georgie, Maxwell, and the students, staff, and families of the Bradford Central School District.